BEST
WOMEN'S
EROTICA

BEST WOMEN'S EROTICA

Edited by

MARCY SHEINER

CLEIS
PRESS

Published in the United States by Cleis Press Inc., P.O. Box 14684, San Francisco, California 94114.

Printed in the United States.

Cover design: Scott Idleman

Cover photo: Phyllis Christopher

Text design: Karen Quigg

Logo art: Juana Alicia

First Edition.

10 9 8 7 6 5 4

"Between the Toes" by Tara Alton was originally published on www.cleansheets.com. "Santa's Little Helper" by Jenesi Ash was originally published in the spring 1999 issue of *Zaftig! Sex for the Well Rounded*. "The Album" by Kate Dominic was originally published in *Herotica #6* (Down There Press, 1999). "Something for the Pain" by Amelia G was originally published in *Blue Blood: The Trade Magazine of Cool*, Issue #7. "Ratatouille" by Susannah Indigo was originally published in *Libido: A Journal of Sex and Sensibility* as well as on the CD *Libido's Best*. "Strange Bedfellows" by Randi Kreger was originally published on www.erotasy.com. "Kali" by Maryanne Mohanraj was originally published on www.cleansheets.com. "Eggs McMenopause" by Lesléa Newman is reprinted from *Girls Will Be Girls: A Novella and Short Stories* by Lesléa Newman (Alyson Publications) and used with permission. "The Instigator" by Lisa Verde was originally published on www.erotasy.com.

CONTENTS

INTRODUCTION:
THE SEX IS NOT THE STORY

RECENTLY I VISITED SOME OLD FRIENDS OF high school vintage and showed them one of my anthologies of women's erotica. The two men in the group began reading sections aloud to one another, tittering and remarking, "This is just like what we used to read in the navy."

Of course I felt crushed, but later on I consoled myself with reality: They had no concept of what's been going on in the world of sex writing for the past decade, and by plucking out "the juicy bits" they failed to notice that the relatively new field of women's erotica does indeed differ from what they "read in the navy." Mind you, I don't think there's anything *wrong* with the jackoff material they read in the navy; it's just that the field of sex writing has evolved significantly over the past decade, and as we enter the new millennium, there's one thing we can say for sure about the state of the art: *The sex is not the story.*

By today's standards, a good erotic story is not merely a description of sexual activity. It isn't a predictable recitation of boy-meets-girl (or girl-meets-girl or boy-meets-boy) and *they did it.* No "wham, bam, thank you ma'am." For me, and for most women writing sexually explicit fiction today—many of whom write "serious" literature as well—the standard is pretty much the same as for any other fiction: plot, character, command of literary craft. The added element is that, while the sex is not the story, it most certainly *is* a central part of any writing that claims to call itself erotica—and for an erotic story to qualify as such, the sex has to be fairly explicit. These are the criteria I've been using for over a decade in writing and editing sexual fiction.

The more difficult question in terms of this collection is, what makes an erotic story qualify as "best"? Again, an engaging plot, believable characters, command of the language, sexual heat—but, for that extra *oomph,* a great or "best" story should have something to say about sex, some revelation, enlightenment, or twist that provokes the reader's mind as well as his or her genitals.

With this in mind, I set out to find the best women's erotica written during the past year, in anthologies, on the Internet, and in first-time submissions. To say that I was not disappointed would be an understatement: I am elated by this collection. Each story is a little jewel, a commentary on sex at the beginning of the new millennium, as well as a good hot read.

Like much of erotica, a fair number of these stories are humorous or ironic; the subject just naturally lends itself to humor. In that category, we've got Santa Claus/fat fetishism ("Santa's Little Helper"), gender-bending ("The Album"), incest fantasies ("Strange Bedfellows"), vegetable sex ("Ratatouille"), menopause ("Eggs McMenopause"), rowdy genderfuck in a dyke bar ("My Kind of Woman"), and the surest escape from the tortures of dentistry that I've ever known ("Something for the Pain"). These stories convey a depth of meaning beyond simply provoking giggles. The writers laugh at the human condition while inviting readers to see themselves as part of the joke. (*Caveat lector:* While most people probably don't read erotica in public places, if you should dare to read "Ratatouille" or "Eggs McMenopause" on the subway, you're bound to attract not just prurient interest, but also stares when you double over laughing and snorting with glee.)

While I love to laugh as much as anyone else, I confess that stories dealing with the darker side of sex are my most guilty pleasure. A few years ago I noted that, for all the female-generated sex writing, women were still avoiding complex issues and feelings that arise during sex, and I urged them to go deeper—which is why I'm so pleased by what emerged for this collection. It has been surprising, and deeply gratifying, that so many of these stories deal with the darker side of sexuality.

It's no coincidence that *Best Women's Erotica 2000* leads off with "Interrogation," a tragicomic satire of the investigation into Bill Clinton's affair with Monica Lewinsky. From the female point of view, we see that the investigation wasn't only about the president of the United States, but about women's still-subservient position in the sexual landscape of this country and how it generated yet more sexual paranoia among the Monicas of the world.

Continuing with dark themes, "Lita" probes the sex/death connection; "Cal's Party" injects revenge into an orgiastic revel; and "Jack's Pride" explores the tricky territory of sex with a returning war hero.

While there's a fair amount of what's called "S/M" in this collection, none of it gets played out in stereotypical dungeon scenes with elaborate equipment—that sort of story is becoming far too predictable and tedious. Instead, the psychological power dynamics underlying S/M are woven into many of these stories. "Service Entrance," for instance, may shock some feminist sensibilities, especially when women find themselves confusingly aroused by its sexual dynamics.

Are women's psyches becoming "evil"? Are women probing deeper inside themselves? Or simply being more honest in their writing? Or, could this just be a reflection of my own editorial bias? Whatever the answer, I've been waiting a long time for women to shed light on the more forbidden corners of our sexuality.

Finally, a few stories in this collection defy categorization into "humor" or "darkness." "Kali" is a Classic Young Dyke Tale; "The Instigator" is a strange twist on a heterosexual relationship; "Arrogance" is the best piece of solo sex I've yet to come across; "Séverine" provides a mesmerizing glimpse into group "marriage"; "Cycles" flawlessly combines humor with grief; and only a woman could have written "Between the Toes," a foot-fetish story that also touches on our time-honored lust for shoes.

Best Women's Erotica represents the debut of a new series. We'll be publishing a collection of the best again next year, and we hope for many years thereafter. If this isn't motivation for women to explore the further reaches of sexuality in their fiction, then I don't know what is.

Marcy Sheiner
Emeryville, California
January 2000

INTERROGATION

IN MY DREAM I'M SITTING AT A TABLE WEARING red socks while my lawyer, a kind man with a soft voice and a plump face whose name is Mr. Marrs, stands in front of me in his navy blue suit and red paisley tie, asking the questions.

"That's Marrs with two r's," he tells me. "I'm not a star," he adds with a chuckle, "but I'll fight for you if you answer my questions honestly."

I feel lucky that he's my lawyer because of his kindness, his obvious desire to put me at ease with his little jokes. We're in a small, white-walled room that Mr. Marrs calls the Interview Room, but I have no idea why I'm being questioned or what I might have done. What view does Mr. Marrs have of my situation? Through the room's only window I see snow drifting from a dark sky.

I

Mr. Marrs has a nice smile, which dimples his plump cheeks and unmasks the straightest, whitest teeth I've ever seen. "This is just a practice session," he explains. "Think of it as a game, like playing catch."

Although it's cold beyond the window where the snow swirls, it's warm in the room because of the bright overhead light that beams down on me like a halo and because of Mr. Marrs's thousand-watt smile, which makes me want to melt in a puddle at his feet, to answer any question he can think of, to tell him what he wants to hear.

"Remember," he says, "this interrogation is off the record. It isn't even a deposition. You're not under oath at the moment, so nothing can be used against you. Shall we begin?"

No one has ever said "shall" to me, and the polite formality of the word almost makes me weep.

He throws the first ball. "Why are you wearing those socks?" he asks, and I tell him that although I really don't know, I could probably come up with a story.

"Probably?" Two dimples appear at the pointed ends of his smile.

He waits while I smile back at him, though we both know my facial dimples aren't nearly as lovely as his. I think it's the dimples on my ass he's after, and on my thighs, which I tighten. The window has disappeared, making the room seem much smaller.

"Have you ever known a Monica?" he asks.

"I've known several," I tell him. "Do you have anyone in particular in mind?"

His tongue flicks between his lips for a second, but he says nothing.

"I don't think I've known a Monica in the sense you mean," I say with what I hope is a saucy smile.

I can see that I've offended him. As he steps back, his smile droops and his dimples disappear. "What sense would that be?" he asks.

2

I look at the floor under the table, at the redness of my socks against the dark blue tile. The room seems to grow colder, as if the light has been turned off, though it still burns above us. For the first time I notice I have nothing else on except those socks, which I pull up as far as I can, thinking they might cover me if only they would stretch far enough.

"I didn't mean..." I start, and then I think, Why should I feel guilty? What have I done? Instead, I toss the question back to him.

"Have *you* ever known a Monica?"

He ignores this, countering instead with another: "And the man who knew her, the—" he consults some notes "—the president, wasn't he? Did you know him, too? Or someone like him?"

I have known presidents of corporations, principals of several schools. "Yes, I have worked for powerful men," I tell him, and he smiles again: the smile that warms the room, the smile that tells me he knows when I'm holding back and approves when I give him the story he wants.

"Tell me what you know, " he says, his face suddenly close to mine.

"OK." I take a deep breath.

He sits down in the empty chair that has appeared on the other side of the table and leans forward, while I decide what to tell him. He moves closer, putting one warm, soft hand on my knee, which he strokes so deftly I moan before I can stop myself. His hand slides up my inner thigh and then withdraws abruptly.

"When are you going to tell me?" he begs, his smile a tease that doesn't quite match the tense blue of his eyes.

"Do you want the truth, or do you want my story?" I ask.

"You aren't under oath," he answers. "Remember what I told you in the beginning. This is just a preliminary quest." Has he interrupted himself, or does he want a search rather than an

answer? His hand slides around to the back of my thigh. I lift
my leg to make it easier for him, and begin:

THE FIRST ENCOUNTER

You could say my moniker is Monica.

(He doesn't react to my pun. His hand continues its climb to
the cleft of my ass, which I raise up off the chair so that his fingers can creep forward into my fur, while the light overhead
seems to whirl, making me dizzy.)

*I've had lots of jobs where Monicas are common. I was a
Monica myself, and I've known several presidents, which is I
suppose why I'm here, in this dream, with only my socks for
cover.*

"What did you do as a Monica?" he asks, breathing deeply.
He's on his knees now, smiling up at me, the light making halos
around both our heads. I wonder if perhaps he'd like to hire me
as his assistant, and decide to make the details as professional
as I can. This could, after all, be a job interview. It's hard to tell
with dreams.

*Monicas do whatever they're required to do: typing, filing,
answering phones, research, scheduling meetings, arranging
travel, delivering papers, just managing everyone's day. We
move from office to office, job to job, title to title: At first we're
File Clerks, then Personal Assistants, Office Managers,
Administrative Aides, Administrative Assistants, Adminis-
trators, but always we make the coffee. We manage.*

"Tell me what you did with him, Monica," Mr. Marrs whispers
from his knees, his warm, wet breath spreading over my belly.

"Him?" I ask. "There were many hims, a range of them."

"You know what I mean," he answers, and he's right, I know
what to tell him.

*We met in the elevator to the 22nd floor, I and the man I
thought was the president of the company where I worked.*

This was my first job: I was the Monica who did filing and photocopying. There in that elevator with ten other people, we locked eyes while everyone else stared politely straight ahead, and from then on, we couldn't resist each other.

Mr. Marrs's hand is patting my damp fur now, his fingers slipping inside me.

We got off the elevator together, walking down the corridor side by side without touching or saying a word, though our minds were in touch. In front of his office he turned to smile at me before going in, his lips forming the name "Monica," which I understood to be an invitation so I followed him in.

"Could you help me with these files?" he asked, but I didn't see any files. I closed the door behind me. He sat down in the chair in front of his desk, the chair he kept for visitors. It was then that I noticed his pants were unzipped, his prick hanging out discreetly, not even hard, just there, flesh against the gray wool, like a hairless pet on his lap.

Mr. Marrs finds my center, the tiny nose sticking up in front of the fur, hardening and becoming more prominent, and gently circles it with his fingertips. My breathing echoes off the bare walls of the room, which seems to have become as small as a closet.

"I love your narrative," he murmurs in my ear before lowering his mouth.

The president smiled at me, spread his legs to let his prick-pet have air to twitch and grow, sit up, left its head, nod.

THE FIRST ORGASM

As it turned out, he wasn't the president of the company, just a junior executive, but that was always my private name for him: The President. He never bothered to learn my real name, either: I was always his Monica. I leapt onto his lap and nestled down. I never wear underpants or pantyhose, just those thigh-highs

with the thick elastic on top that almost cuts off your circula-
tion. My toes may have been numb, but my cunt and my clit
were both humming as I guided his pet inside my fur, leaning
my free hand on the back of the chair. He gasped as we began
to move up and down together. My clit rubbed against the loose
zipper of his pants, the pressure of hard metal more arousing
than painful, until I began to feel a warm glow all up inside that
made my toes quiver. When I felt him twitch in me, felt his flow
of liquid heat, I realized too late that this really wasn't exactly a
safe thing to be doing, but then I thought, it's all right, he's the
president (which he wasn't), and anyway this is all a tale I'm
telling in a dream. Was I wrong?

Mr. Marrs is on his knees before me, his soft full lips around
my clit, tongue lapping like a little dog, and even though this is
hardly professional, I'm so excited I rise off my chair, my feet in
their red socks straining to keep me balanced. As my hips hit
the edge of the table, Mr. Marrs grabs my thighs and forces me
to sit again, holding me in place while his tongue twists and
swirls, while my chair thumps as I move up and down,
restrained only by his hand. Waves of a hot ocean wash over
me, hot enough to steam the windows (if there were any).
When I lay my head on the table, panting, Mr. Marrs pats my
knee and then crawls out to sit in the other chair, licking his lips
and smoothing his thin hair back with one hand while he picks
up his pen with the other.

"Go on," he urges.

THE SECOND ORGASM

The president tried to rouse me right away, shaking my shoul-
der while pulling my hair. "Hey," he said, "hey, we have to be
careful here; someone might come in."

He was still hard inside me, moving slowly, a man already
satisfied, poking and prodding inside me for a repeat. He

heaved me onto his desk, scattering pens and papers, one of those dream transportations where you wonder, How did I get here? Fly? And with him still inside me? But there I was, flat on my back, the blotter bunched under my right shoulder, his prick edging deep inside me until, yes, I felt another response building, slowly, quietly, until it popped like a slightly flat bottle of bargain champagne. He was still at it, standing behind the desk with his pants down around his ankles while I twisted around, trying to move my shoulder off that blotter, but I only managed to get a pen or something under my spine.

"Oh man oh man," the president whispered in my ear so loud and breathy I was afraid someone in the hall might hear him. Finally, with a loud grunt, he finished.

Mr. Marrs squirms in his chair like a restless little boy. "Is there more?" he asks. "Is there more?"

"Well, I guess," I tell him. "I worked there six months."

"Tell me about your mouth," he says.

THE THIRD ORGASM

It was in the photocopy room. I was running off a pile of legal documents when he came in with this one little thing he wanted to copy, so I let him, because after all that we'd done, he had privileges, even if it did mean I had to change the paper from legal to regular. I let him slide into the narrow room behind me and rub against my rump as he reached over to close and lock the door. I plucked the letter he wanted copied from his fingers, put it into the feeder, and pressed Print. He turned me around by my shoulders and kissed me while the copy machine flashed and groaned behind us, hiding any disturbance we might make.

Because I couldn't move any way but up or down, I slid down until I was on my knees, my face at his crotch, my fingers on his zipper, which hissed and possibly ripped as I pulled it down so that I could unfold his dick from the wrapping of his trousers and underwear.

He wasn't hard, which shocked me because we hadn't known each other long enough to get that bored. It was more work than I'd anticipated to disentangle a limp penis from its coverings, to massage it with my fingertips, suck and lick it, but slowly it came to life as my mouth surrounded it while he stood facing the copy machine. If anyone had come in they probably wouldn't have noticed me crouched between his knees.

He swayed his hips back and forth while stapling his copies and stacking them neatly on top of the machine. I just followed him with my mouth.

Mr. Marrs leans back from the table, thrusting his hips forward. "And then?" he breathes. "Did he come?" He puts his hands casually into his pockets, his two forefingers pointing directly to the dog I know must be twitching impatiently beneath the zipper, ready for a walk.

Well, I could hardly tell when he came. Maybe he sighed just before he suddenly went all limp, as I found myself swallowing globs of cum down my throat, which I usually like to avoid doing by pulling away at the last moment and letting guys shoot in my hand or breast or down my dress or anywhere, I don't care, I just don't like the taste of it, that day-old fish with rotting, garlic bread bouquet. The president tasted like stale bread with rancid butter, not the worst I've had but not something I'd recommend, either.

Mr. Marrs looks disappointed, leaning back in his chair, frowning a little as he sucks his lower lip, his fingers still pointing to his zipper, which glints in the folds of his pants. He looks at me and then looks around the room at the blank walls that seal us in.

"Were there any gifts?" he asks.

THE GIFTS

Yes, of course we brought little things to work for each other, mostly lunch food. I gave him pasta salad with sardines. Then I read how you can change the taste of a man's semen by what you feed him, so I only brought sweet things: cookies, cupcakes, cream puffs. It didn't work, but I eventually got used to his taste. He gave me a pink-and-orange troll to set on top of my computer, a pencil with a pumpkin on it for Halloween, and a pink eraser that glowed in the dark.

When I went to Hawaii with my girlfriend, I bought him a T-shirt that said "Keep on surfin'" across the front. That's what we used to call it when he went down on me: surfin'. When I did it to him, it was fishin' with his pole in my mouth.

Mr. Marrs leans forward. I can feel his warm breath, which smells of milk, of chocolate, of cinnamon.

"How often did you go fishing?" he asks.

Once a day, at least, he'd request a file from the file room—and when it was something about fish, or surf, or Hawaii, or anything at all to do with the ocean, Liz, the file supervisor, would bring it to me to take to him. I think now that he must have told her to do that. Anyway, I'd take it right up and he'd lock the door to his office and I'd go down on my knees, unzip him, and—well, it gets repetitive. Mr. Marrs?

He's down on his knees now, as though he's begging, head in my fur, tongue routing around until he finds my clit and grabs it with his lips. I think of surfboards cresting waves, and shout as I hit the big one, crashing and falling to shore. My legs rise up and kick the table, almost tipping it over.

"Careful, careful," says Mr. Marrs as he gets up with his hands on his head. "Were there trips?"

What's the difference between trips and gifts? I wonder if this is a foul ball, a trick question, a way to find out whether I'll demand travel funds if he hires me as his assistant.

THE TRIPS

He didn't take me many places because he had a wife and family, even a dog, and he didn't want any of them to see me acciden-tally. He did take me to Alaska once, though, to look at an oil rig. The company was paying for him and his Personal Assistant, who didn't want to go, so he asked me instead. We flew up to the North Pole (so we joked, because it was December, just before Christmas) and spent a couple of days in a hotel, which I never left. He went out alone and came back at night, when we'd have dinner in the café on the first floor and then go up to bed, where he'd impale me on his own north pole all night.

We were there two nights, and I don't think he slept at all. I slept all day. We didn't wear anything but our socks because our feet were cold no matter how high we turned up the heat, internal and external. That's Alaska for you. His dick was always hard—the magnetic influence of the North Pole, he said, ha-ha. Sometimes I'd hang stuff on it: a scarf, a necklace, a bracelet, but I never gave him any of those things because they were mine, and they weren't gifts, either—they were things I'd bought for myself. I did give him a pair of white socks with a blue Sourdough's face on them: you know, that bearded prospector who's the symbol of Alaska. And he gave me red wool socks, these socks I have on now, which he called my Santa Claus socks.

I lift my foot so that Mr. Marrs can admire them. "You men-tioned his wife," he said. "Did she find out about you? Was she angry at you?

WIVES

Wives are never angry at me—it's their husbands who piss them off, usually just in general. The president's wife was a lawyer who worked for the government. He had a first wife, too, the mother of his son and daughter, who were grown, who even had kids of their own, so he was already a grandfather, though he didn't look it. He said the dog was his wife's dog, but he didn't say which wife.

Both his wives used to call him at the office and say, "This is his wife," as though there could be no confusion. His Personal Assistant never knew which wife it was, so she'd just tell him his wife was on the phone, and he'd pick up as if there was no problem at all. I think he was intrigued by the mystery, like not knowing exactly who's getting in bed with you. He used to like me to wear a mask in bed so that he wouldn't be sure it was me. I suppose those masks were gifts, too, since I still have them. There was one made of peacock feathers that covered just my eyes, and one of a pig's face, with a bow between the ears, and a really foxy Siamese cat face.

Mr. Marrs is pacing back and forth in front of the table now, clearing his throat. Finally he says, "How did it end, assuming it did? Let's discuss completion."

THE END

Oh, it ended, all right. Maybe his wives found out or he found another Monica—several new ones were hired, soft young things, though not nearly as qualified as I was by then, but who cares about quality? Or maybe I just got bored with the job, with him, with everything. I left the company, and didn't see him as often. At first he would call, but that happened less and less. I was angry, but not all that angry because I already had a better job as a Personal Assistant to another man, an Assistant Manager who had no wives so was a much better prospect as far as marriage goes, because the aim of all Monicas is permanence, you know, which is why we're always changing jobs and boyfriends.

Mr. Marrs sits down in his chair, leaning forward, elbows on the table, which I'd always been taught was rude, but maybe that's just at dinner. I wait for his next question, but he says nothing, just folds his plump hands on the table while smiling his porcelain smile until I catch his meaning. I slide under the table and crawl over to him on my knees, taking his zipper in my teeth, pulling it down until his cock unfurls from his pants like one of those dark, mysterious plants, a jack-in-the-pulpit or a peony, that seem like part of the earth when they sprout.

I know that I owe this to him; in my dream I'm glad to pay anything for my defense, though for *what* I'm still not sure. Or maybe I'm paying for the possibility of a better job. Whatever it is, the price seems about right. I bend down to this flower, lowering my mouth onto its musky stalk, sliding its bloom around in my mouth. I think of nipping at it, but he might not like that, so I limit myself to sucking and sliding, opening my throat to it until he moans and calls out, "Did he ever feel like this, was he this hard, this big, did he punch the back of your throat, did he blow your ears out when he came?"

I can't answer these questions, of course, since my mouth is full; all I can manage is an "Uh-hum," until he cries out, "Yes, yes yes yes," rising up from the table, kicking the chair, dragging me with him, my mouth still in place, still working. I can almost taste something like his breath, a milky sweetness; I think he'll be the first tasty man I've ever had, but he pulls away to leave us both sitting at the table again, with a door open and the window back in place so that I can see that the snow has melted in the sun.

He says, "I think you've done very well," his teeth gleaming more than they had at night.

I look down to see if he's still hard, but of course I can't see through the table, so I look at myself and notice I'm now wearing a gray-and-navy striped suit with a blue silk blouse that matches his eyes. Mr. Marrs stands up, shakes my hand, and then says, with his glittering smile, "Thank you very much. We'll call you."

When I stand up, I see that my red socks are gone, and in their place are stockings, worn with a pair of black high-heeled shoes. I nod my head, I say, "Thank you, it's been very interesting talking to you," and then I tiptoe out the door into the waking world.

SERVICE ENTRANCE

Kristina Wright

SHE WAS LATE. JENNIFER GLANCED AT HER watch as she passed under a streetlight. She walked a little faster, her heels clicking on the sidewalk, pounding out some strange code only she understood. A light breeze chilled her skin.

It was after midnight, but there was a steady flow of traffic. She kept her head down and turned away from the street. Her car was in a parking garage four blocks away. She wasn't likely to run into anyone she knew in this part of town, but it never hurt to be careful. She was always careful.

She was a little breathless when she finally rounded the corner and saw the bar. The smell of liquor hung heavy in the air, and the steady, pounding beat of rock music drifted out. She slipped into the alley as two men staggered out the front door. She took a deep breath, trying to steady her nerves before tapping on the service door.

The door opened immediately, as if he'd been waiting there for her. "You're late," he said, wrapping his fingers around her wrist and pulling her into the dimly lit bar. She wondered if he could feel the rapid beat of her pulse.

"I know." She took another breath, hoping he wouldn't send her away. "I'm sorry."

He studied her face for a minute and then nodded toward the office door. "Let's go."

The office was small, cramped, with room for little more than a desk and a filing cabinet. Papers covered the desktop, and an open bottle of whiskey sat on the filing cabinet. He closed the door, cutting off the noise from the bar. She shivered.

"Want a drink?"

She shook her head. "No, thank you."

His quiet laugh slid over her like a touch. "No, you don't come here to drink. At least not from a bottle."

His words made her wet. She didn't bother to disagree with him.

"Nice jacket," he said, running his fingers over the fur collar of her coat. "What are you wearing underneath?"

She dropped her eyes, suddenly shy. She didn't know why. It wasn't as if this was the first time she'd come to him.

He leaned against the desk, arms crossed over his chest. "Show me, Jenny."

She met his gaze. His eyes were the same amber color as the whiskey bottle. "Why do you call me that?" No one ever called her Jenny.

He reached out and rubbed his thumb across her bottom lip, tugging at it gently. "Because that's who you are. Now, show me what you're wearing, Jenny."

She reached for the belt of her coat and fumbled with the knot. When it came undone, she let the coat slide off her shoulders and pool at her feet. She was naked except for the black silk stockings and black high heels that she wore only for him. She wondered if looking at her body aroused him as much as exposing herself to his gaze aroused her. She lowered her head again, waiting for his response. She saw herself through his eyes: firm, pale breasts and a flat stomach; a dark triangle of curls above long, shapely legs.

"Well now," he said, his voice low and familiar. "Jenny's not wearing much at all tonight."

Her skin grew hot. He stroked his fingers across her hardened nipples. They tightened and she pressed her thighs together.

He didn't miss the move. He made a tsking sound in his throat. "Impatient?"

She nodded.

"Good. I like that." He ran his hands over her shoulders and she fought to keep still. "You'll be begging before I'm through. You know that, don't you?"

A little moan escaped her throat. "Yes."

"And that's what you want, isn't it?"

She nodded.

He resumed his caress down her arms, across her breasts that felt heavy and sensitive, down her waist to her stomach. "Are you wet, Jenny?"

She nodded, though she hated admitting that he could arouse her with so little contact. Hell, she had been aroused before she'd even gotten here.

"I can smell your cunt." His fingers tangled in her pubic hair. "Maybe next time you'll shave this for me."

It wasn't a question. She knew she'd shave herself bare for him. "Yes."

A burst of laughter from the bar stilled his fingers. "I don't have much time. On your knees, Jenny."

She dropped to her knees in front of him, and he twisted his fingers in her long hair. She resisted the temptation to press her mouth against the bulge in his pants. Her knees hurt from the hard floor and her shoes pinched her toes, but she waited for him to tell her what to do.

He tugged at her hair, tilting her head up. "Unzip my pants."

She reached up with trembling fingers and did as he said. The zipper sounded loud in the quiet room. His breath came a little quicker as she eased the zipper over his hardness. She caught a glimpse of skin and realized he wasn't wearing underwear. It thrilled her.

"Good girl. Now take it out."

She unfastened the button on his pants and freed his cock, breathing in his scent. He was big, bigger than she remembered. Bigger than she'd ever had. She held his cock in one hand and cupped his balls with the other. Her pussy got wetter as she touched him.

He was so beautiful, so hard. His cock was dark pink and engorged. She liked to think the inside of her pussy was this same color, that they were cut from the same cloth. She stroked the length of his penis, testing the weight of him, feeling the iron strength beneath the velvety soft skin. She moaned low in her throat and squeezed her thighs together.

His fingers tightened in her hair. "You could do this for another man, for a hundred other men, but no one will ever make you feel the way I do."

She didn't know why he said that. Maybe because he wanted to believe she belonged to him. Right now, for this moment, she did.

A drop of fluid clung to the head of his cock. She swiped her tongue over the plump tip and licked it away. His cock jumped in her hand as if it had a mind of its own, and she squeezed it hard. His cock wept another tear for her. She licked him again and again, until he couldn't stand it any longer.

He was pulling her hair hard now. "Suck it, Jenny. Suck it."

She licked her lips, wetting them so that he'd slide in easily. Then she took the head of his cock into her mouth. It nestled on the hollow of her tongue, as if it were meant to be there. He groaned and thrust his hips forward, forcing more of his shaft into her mouth. She wanted to touch herself, but her hands and her mouth were full of him.

He let her do the work, leaning against the desk, hands resting lightly on the back of her head. She took him deep into her throat—she'd been working on that—and then pulled back all the way to the head. Down, up, down, up, creating a rhythm that had nothing to do with the music filtering in from the jukebox.

She pulled her mouth off him and replaced it with her hands as she trailed her tongue down the length of his cock and over his heavy, hairy testicles. He groaned as she sucked first one, then the other, into her mouth. His cock pressed against her cheek, wet from her saliva. She loved the musky scent of him against her face.

He covered her hands with one of his own and stroked himself as she licked and sucked his balls. "Touch yourself."

She sat back on her heels and looked up at him. She cupped her breasts in her hands, offering them up to him. "Like this?"

He nodded, his hand moving faster on his cock. "More."

She pinched her nipples hard, pulled them out from her breasts, and let them go. Then she licked her fingers slowly, sliding them into her mouth as if she was sucking him, before rubbing them over her nipples.

"Touch your cunt. I want to hear how wet you are."

She did as he told her, slipping her hands down over her stomach and between her damp thighs. Her pussy made a liquid sucking sound when she slid two fingers inside it, as if she was filled with hot oil.

"I hear you," he whispered, his gaze locked with hers. "You're so wet for me, for my cock."

She nodded.

"Beg me for it."

She tried to speak, but her words barely came out as a whisper. "Please let me taste you. I want you to come in my mouth. Please."

He pointed his cock at her. "Then suck me, Jenny. Make me come."

She leaned forward, taking his cock in her mouth while fucking herself with her fingers and rubbing her clit with the palm of her hand. She used her other hand to stroke his cock into her mouth, running her tongue over and around the head before sucking it between her lips like a ripe plum. She looked up and saw him watching her.

He guided her head with his hand. "You're going to come, aren't you?"

She could only nod. She would come when he did. She heard his breathing change and knew it wouldn't be long. She sucked him deeper into her mouth, working her tongue, even her teeth, over his cock. She stirred the wetness in her pussy into a froth, feeling the need building inside her. She wanted to scream her orgasm around the cock in her mouth.

His hand returned to his cock, holding it while she sucked. "Now, Jenny," he gasped.

Her pussy contracted around her fingers as the first splash of his cum hit the back of her throat. She swallowed without ever tasting it. She moaned, nearly doubled over with the sensation of the orgasm in her pussy and the orgasm he was having in her mouth. She slid her lips down to the head of his cock and savored the taste of him.

He pulled out of her mouth and came on her lips and her cheeks. She knelt there, rocking on her hand as her orgasm peaked and began to subside. He finished painting her face and mouth with his semen and sagged heavily against the desk.

She leaned into him. She would leave a wet spot on the front of his dark trousers, but she didn't care. His cock brushed her cheek and she kissed it affectionately. She watched it shrink and knew she had satisfied him. Her pussy still contracted around her fingers, as little ripples of pleasure emanated from that spot deep inside her.

He shifted after a few moments and she sat back. Her fingers made a wet sound as they slid out of her pussy and heat rushed to her cheeks. Passion satiated, she could be embarrassed again, shy about her performance. She looked up at him and saw something raw and vulnerable in his expression. Or maybe it was only a reflection of what she felt.

"I have to get back up front." He tucked his cock back into his pants and zipped up before helping her to her feet.

She started to wipe the wetness from her face, but he held her hands. "No, leave it. You can clean up when you get home. I want you to remember me." He picked up her coat and belted it around her, concealing her nakedness.

"I'd better be going," she whispered. She reached into her pocket and pulled out a folded hundred-dollar bill. She handed it to him. "Thank you."

He hesitated only a minute before putting the money in his pocket. "I don't understand you."

For the first time since she'd arrived, she smiled. "You understand me better than anyone. You know who I am."

"Maybe I do. Next Friday, then?"

She shook her head. "I can't. I'm hosting a dinner party for my husband's colleagues. Saturday night? Please?"

He chuckled. "Saturday night."

She let out a breath she didn't know she'd been holding. "Good."

He walked her to the back door, not touching her. She stepped out into the alley, feeling the air on her skin and the dampness between her thighs and on her face.

"Jenny?"

She glanced over her shoulder at his silhouette in the darkened doorway. "Yes?"

"Come early, Saturday."

She licked her lips, tasting him again. "I will."

LITA

Cara Bruce

IT WAS RAINING AGAIN. I SAT IN MY THIRD-STORY room and stared out the window. If this didn't stop soon I was going to lose my mind, I was sure of it. It had been almost two months since my last lover had moved out, and it had been raining ever since.

I sighed and walked to the window to close the shades. Just as I began to draw the heavy linen curtain, I noticed my neighbors across the street. The woman was topless, with her face and chest pressed against the glass, and the man was behind her, his large hands reaching around and caressing her breast, his mouth planting kisses on the slender curve of her neck. The rain was beating in slanted sheets upon the window, almost creating a screen for the lovers. I moved the curtain so that only one eye was peeking out.

I could almost feel when the man entered her. The woman's entire body was heaved upward, hard against the glass. I could now see that she was completely naked, her legs spread. One of the man's hands was wrapped tightly around her waist, the other moving up and over her clit. Her head lolled from side to side in orgiastic pleasure. I could almost imagine the moans that were escaping her lips, and my body quivered. I slipped my hand down the front of my silk pajama bottoms, feeling the cool fabric on one side and the hot breath of my cunt on the other. My fingers grazed over my patch of curly hairs and gently parted the swelling lips of my labia. The lovers across the street were still going at it, and I let the curtain fall away, sure they wouldn't notice me in the midst of their revelry.

I drew a finger across my nipple, making it harden. Lightly I pinched it, gently pulling it outward. My pussy was beginning to drip. I stroked my clit, letting that grow as well. My legs felt weak. I rubbed myself and watched as the man thrust into the woman across the street. He lifted his hand and dragged a finger across her mouth. Her tiny hands were balled into fists that beat against the window and I could practically hear her screaming with pleasure.

Quickly I slipped off my pajamas, the cool air hardening my nipples until I thought they would pop off. I stood there completely naked, my legs spread like the woman's across the street, except that instead of him behind me I had my own hand working its magic. At this point I wanted them to see me; I was sure they wouldn't care, and I almost needed them to know how much I was enjoying their spectacle.

The rain picked up, so hard that it almost provided complete coverage. I matched my frenzied flicking with the sound of the battering drops against the glass. My legs were tightening and I was about to get myself off when the sound of breaking glass and a piercing scream shot through the air.

I squinted my eyes and the rain seemed to break for a second. The window across the street was shattered into a million pieces and the man was standing there, naked, still half-hard, his arms empty and his mouth frozen open. He looked up at me. Our eyes locked for one second before he turned and ran out of the room.

I looked down to the street at the woman. Her long hair was soaked, one arm twisted upward and the other one stuck to her side. Her neck was turned so that the right side of her face was plastered to the pavement.

Hurriedly I put on my pajamas. I glanced down once more, in time to see the man running down the street. I sprinted down the stairs of my apartment and out to her. I no longer felt myself breathing; I felt as if I had stepped out of my body.

The woman's face was frozen in orgiastic rapture. Its twisted comicalness sent shivers up my spine. Other neighbors were coming out of their houses, and in the distance of the morning I could hear the faint whir of sirens. I knelt down in the wet and blood-stained street. All I could think about was how sorry I was that everyone had to see her like this, soaking wet and broken. How incredibly beautiful she had looked just moments before, making love against the window.

I slipped back inside my building and up to my apartment. I sat in the window and watched them cover her body and take it away, the white sheet clinging to her beautiful figure in the rain. The police were in her apartment, placing shards of glass into tiny plastic bags. I just sat there until one of them looked up, right into my eyes, as I knew he would. A few minutes later he was knocking at my door.

The officer was young and good-looking. He asked the basic questions, and I told him what I had seen. I told him about the sex, the way the newly deceased woman had been pressed up against the window, how her chest had heaved, how her hair had gotten caught in her mouth, how the rain had been falling.

My officer was becoming a little flustered, his face growing red and his pants beginning to bulge. Even with the thought of her on the pavement, I was getting slightly aroused myself.

"Are those all the questions?" I asked him.

"Yes, for now." He handed me his card, "If you think of anything, call me." I took the card and smiled, glad he didn't wink.

Two days passed, and I heard nothing. I spent most of those days staring out the window and watching people going through her apartment, watching the street cleaners brush up the million pieces of sparkling glass, watching the white chalk drawing slowly fade into the pavement. I even walked across the street and looked at her mailbox to try and learn her name. It said "L. Morano," written in an almost childish scrawl. I wondered how old she was. The end of the second day, someone—it must have been her mother—came and gathered up clothing, books, and knickknacks. I sat on my couch and watched her, shoulders slumped, burdened by her grief. There was a part of me that wished to call out to her, to take her in my arms and comfort her. By this point, I was more than intrigued, I was obsessed. And through it all no one thought to close the shades. I began to suspect the dead woman had had none.

That night I lay in bed and tried to sleep. Guilt crept over me: Every time I closed my eyes I could see strands of her wet hair stuck to her face on the street, and that awful, horrific image triggered a sexual response in me so great that I was compelled to put my hands between my legs and attempt to get myself off. But no matter how much I tried, I could not achieve release, and eventually I would get tired and stop. My only comforting thought was that I was not Catholic—if I was, I would surely be permanently fucked in the head and in therapy forever.

But one night when I lay in my bed after my third failed attempt at masturbation, I heard a knock at my door. I knew it was going to be him. I put on a robe and opened the door. There stood the man from across the street. His eyes were bloodshot and his hands were trembling. I stepped aside and let him in.

He stood for a second looking out my window, imagining what I must have seen, probably remembering the feel of her hair against his face, her heaving tit in his hand, her hot cunt clenching around his hard cock. His breath quickened, and he turned to face me. Silently I slipped out of my robe, letting it puddle around my feet on the floor. He took a step toward me, lifting his T-shirt off his body. His eyes traveled over me, lingering on each curve for that seductive second that makes one's blood boil.

His mouth pressed down upon mine. His lips were strong and his hand held the back of my neck. My fingers groped with the buttons of his jeans, releasing his cock so that it sprang out hard as a rod. He stepped out of his jeans and bent his neck until his mouth was on my tit, his warm tongue licking over my nipple; his fingers almost viciously grabbed a handful of flesh. He lifted me up, settling my pussy on his cock. I was tight for his entrance, his hands grabbing onto my ass as he lifted and lowered me. I wrapped my long legs around his waist and twisted my fingers through his hair. He pounded into me, thrusting and pumping, fucking me hard and fast. I tossed my head back and pretended I was the woman. I began to moan, and he entered me harder and faster. I looked over his shoulder and out the window, half expecting to see somebody there.

"Lita," he groaned. I pulled his face to the curve in my neck.

"Fuck me the way you were fucking her," I whispered.

He lowered us to the floor and held my hands over my head. His cock rammed into my quivering cunt, and I felt my body on the urge of a breakthrough.

"I'm about to die," I said.

He thrust in deeper.

"The window is going to shatter and I'm going to be lying dead on the pavement." I couldn't help myself; I knew it was twisted, but it was turning me on. He grabbed my hair and harshly tugged.

"My hair is going to be soaking wet, plastered to my face," I whispered in his ear, imagining the orgiastic grin it would be hiding.

Suddenly he picked up the pace and was fucking me hard and fast, as if his life depended on it. My hips lifted and my pussy began to spasm; my legs shook and tightened under him and I came. He thrust hard into me one more time, and then pulled out and shot his hot, white load all over my stomach.

He collapsed on top of me, in a crying, quivering heap.

I held him until the indigo sky began to melt into violet. He got up, dressed, and left. I put my robe back on and stared out the window, watching as the last of the season's rain washed away the remains of her ghostly chalk outline underneath my window.

THE INSTIGATOR

Lisa Verde

"Oh, Jesus, not your hair again."

"Yes, my hair. Don't you think it's lost its curl?" I pushed it off the back of my neck with my hand. "It used to be bouncy."

"It's winter. Maybe you need humidity."

I nodded. "Maybe.

"Great," said Mike, flipping pages in his magazine. "Then can we stop talking about it?"

"Yeah, sure," I said. I tapped my pen on the coffee table. "Maybe I could get a perm."

"Fine."

"Fine? All you're going to say is fine? I can completely change my look and this has no effect on you whatsoever?"

"None."

"Fine," I said. I crossed my arms and sat back on the couch. This was hardly satisfying. "When are *you* going to get a haircut, then?"

Mike ran his hand through his hair without looking up. "I don't know what you mean," he grumbled.

"Oh, all right, never mind. It looks good," I said. Mike put the magazine down on the table and raised his eyebrows at me.

"Really, Mike, it looks good. I just thought you said you were going to get one."

"When did I say that?" he asked.

"At Marie's house last Saturday."

"And you said it was fine."

"It *is* fine. I said it looks good. It's just a little long—you know, around your ears."

"You want me to get my hair cut."

"No, I don't," I shook my head. "That's not what I mean at all. But if you want to do it, that would be cool. I was just reminding you."

"Because you want me to."

"I just told you: if you want to, that's cool, because it's just a little long. But if you're happy with it, then leave it."

"No, Claire. See, I don't care either way. Get a haircut or not—makes no difference to me. But *you* care, right? That's why you're asking?"

"You don't have to get that way."

"So if you want me to do it, then I will. Why don't you just say what you mean?"

"Geez, it's no big deal. Calm down."

He leaned forward in his chair. "Do you want me to get one or not?"

"It really doesn't matter to me."

"Christ!" He slapped his hands on his bare thighs, leaving two instant red marks on the stubble. I'd asked him to shave his legs for me last week, and his skin was still sensitive and ticklish. He said it itched terribly at work, and I enjoyed the thought of him trying to keep still during those long meetings. Concentrating on each pore in his legs.

Concentrating on a desire to wriggle in his seat to satisfy an unreachable itch.

I liked knowing that it itched and kept him thinking of me. Reminding him of me all day and, I presumed, reminding him of the affection I gave him for doing it. He said it was too uncomfortable to do often. I thought he wasn't paying enough attention to maintaining it. The stubble chafed the insides of my legs. I asked him to do it more frequently, and he complained that it burned and left a rash. He liked it enough, though, when my tongue was tracing long lines from the back of his knees to the crease below his buttocks.

He rubbed his legs where the red marks had come up. "Jesus, Claire. When is this going to get better?"

"You have to do it a lot."

"This was a terrible idea."

"I like it." I grinned at his hands on his legs. "Do you want me to get you some oil?"

"No."

"I'll be right back," I said, and got up from the couch. I walked to him and slapped the hand on his thigh. He was caught off-guard, and for a moment looked angry. I shook my head. "Stop scratching," I said. "You'll only make it worse."

I thought ahead; I couldn't help it. First I would rub oil down his thighs, and then into his heels. I would press my knuckles into his calves and nose gently at the tops of his thighs. He loves that. His dick is heavy and brown, really sensitive. Gentle stroking through his clothes makes him thick, makes his arms relax and his breath even. He puts his head back. If I reach up and twist his nipples gently, I can get him to gasp. That's my goal. To make him gasp.

I know he likes it when I make him wait, so I puttered around the bathroom for a few minutes. I got the oil from the drawer, and then took out the glass cleaner and sprayed the mirror. The smell of ammonia gets me hot. It's weird, but true.

Probably has something to do with my upbringing. When I put the glass cleaner back I noticed that my nail polish was chipped. I took the polish remover from the shelf and pressed a cotton-ball to the opening. The liquid was cold on my fingertips as I rubbed the polish off. The smell of acetone was overpowering and gave me an instant headache. I flipped the switch for the fan; it began rattling and roaring over my head. I wanted to do a nice job and thought I should file my nails, maybe paint them again, but I couldn't get the image of Mike's swelling dick out of my head. It's beautiful, huge and meaty. Looking at it strikes something deep in my lizard brain and makes me want to kill that woolly mammoth and fry it up in a pan. Makes me want to bear him 15 children and live out my days licking his toes in supplication.

Suddenly he appeared in the doorway of the bathroom, and he looked pissed.

"I said, what the hell are you doing in here?"

"I didn't hear you."

"Well, why is the fan on?"

"This stuff gives me a headache."

He snorted in frustration. I sort of half-hoped he would slap his thighs again.

"I'm going to bed," he said, and walked down the hall.

"I'll be right there," I called after him.

I like him when he's angry. He comes really hard, fucking me from behind with his hands digging into my shoulders for leverage, and biting the back of my neck. I have to beg him, literally beg him, to reach down for my clit while he humps my ass.

But sometimes I'll push him too far and he refuses to fuck me at all. I have to whine and tickle him, roll over on top of him and ride his hip for a minute to get him started. If that doesn't work, it takes a few hard bites to the tip of his cock before he'll slap me on the ass to make me quit. That slap gets him going, though, and he'll fuck me then just for spite.

I thought again about his legs: now that they were shaven I could see the divots and crevices between his muscles. The hard fists of muscle in his thighs. The twist of his tibias, going down to his ankles, which are slightly inflexible for a man his age, but shapely. Also, because he had oiled his skin to relieve some of the itch, the smoothness of it made me want to do things like press my nipples against the backs of his knees, or lick his shins, or rub my clit against his knee with his dick in my mouth, until I could nearly come.

I couldn't dawdle any more so I put the polish remover away, pushing the polish bottles around with my finger to make room on the shelf. I thought I'd use that grape color next time I did my nails and toenails. Mike has nice toes, but he's so tense that he keeps them off the ground when he walks around barefoot. The sinews draw straight, taut lines across the tops of his feet. When he sits he keeps them curled under as if he's afraid someone might spring up in front of him and stomp right on them. It took me a long time to love those toes.

I held the bottle of grape polish in my hand.

"Claire!"

This time I could hear him over the sound of the fan, which meant he was near the end of his rope. I grabbed the oil off the counter and turned off the light. Mike was lying on the bed with his arms crossed and his forearms over his eyes. He raised his arms and looked at me.

"Can we please go to bed now?"

"Sure, baby," I said sweetly.

He peered at me. His hair curled handsomely over his forehead.

"What's in your hand?"

"The oil." I held it out to him. "I told you, you should moisturize a lot."

"No, Claire, in your other hand."

I looked down. I still had the grape polish. "This?" I said. Why did I still have it? "This is for you."

"Claire, really, I'm tired." He put his arms over his face again. "I'll paint your nails tomorrow, OK?"

"OK," I said, and got on the bed, facing away from him and sitting on his knees, pinning his legs to the down quilt.

"Hey," he said crossly. "What are you doing?"

I didn't turn around. I reached down and pinched his big toe between my forefinger and thumb, pressing my thumb flat against the nail. I remembered the first time I'd rubbed his feet, licked the thin pink skin between his toes, bit hard into his heels.

"Claire?"

Then there was another time I had been kneading his ankles, kneeling on the floor beneath him while he sat on the edge of the bed. He groaned and leaned back, cupping his balls in his hand and pinching the skin. I got the bright idea to help him out—I got up on my knees, pressed my tongue under his scrotum, and licked that bevel of flesh between his balls and asshole. He moaned and twitched inadvertently, bumping his big toe into my clit. I caught his foot between my thighs and as I speared his asshole with my tongue I rode his foot as if it was my new best friend.

"Claire, what are you doing?"

"Nothing, honey," I said, unscrewing the top of the polish bottle. "Go to sleep."

Mike sighed and tried to roll over, and then grumbled ill-temperedly when he realized his legs were immobilized. I wriggled my ass on his knees.

"Cute, baby. Now come on. Get off me."

"No," I said, and stroked the brush against the side of the bottle opening to get the excess off. The color was a very dark purple, his favorite. It would look delicious against his deep brown skin. Like candy.

First I leaned down and pushed my tongue into the space between his big toe and the next one. Mike gasped, then sighed.

I rested my weight on my elbows and dipped the brush into the bottle again.

"That felt really good," Mike murmured. "Your ass looks great."

"Thanks, baby," I said, stroking the brush on top of the bottle.

"Hold still now."

"What?"

"I said hold still. Can you do that for me?"

"Uh, yeah."

I looked at the tip of the brush. A drop of polish was slowly sliding down the rod, then onto the bristles. I waited until it slid to the tip and then touched it to Mike's left big toenail. He shivered.

"What are you doing?"

The drop was almost perfectly round, fatter on the bottom because of the angle. I dipped the brush again and brought it back to his toenail, full of paint, so that I would have enough to get a good coat. It was wet and shiny, and it spread easily. I stroked slowly from the cuticle to the tip.

"Claire, what are you doing?"

"I'm painting your nails."

"Why?"

"Just keep still."

The next nail was smaller, and the rest smaller still, so they weren't as satisfying, didn't feel as gluttonous. For his smallest toe I used too much paint, and the color beaded and shone like a jewel.

"Claire, that's enough. Take that stuff off of me."

"No."

"Come on. You had your fun."

"I'm not done yet."

He bucked his knees up sharply under my ass and threw me off balance. "I said, get off me. Hey! I can't believe you did that. I look like a fag, Claire." He tried to get off the bed, and I threw my weight back over his hips. "Shave my legs and paint my nails: cute. Get off me now. I mean it."

"No."

"Dammit, Claire!" He slapped my ass. I was looking at him over my shoulder and saw him bite his lower lip at the sound of the slap.

"They're mine, right?" I said. "The whole package is supposed to be mine. Right?"

"Yeah," he muttered.

"Not just your dick, right?" He nodded. "Well, then, keep still."

I could hear him breathing hard and petulantly through his nose as I turned around and went back to work on his other foot. My weight was back on my elbows so my ass was again facing him, only now it felt exposed and it tingled from that slap. I could feel him staring at it. I took the brush out again and prepared to paint the nails on his other foot. Mike wiggled his knees. "Baby, take your panties off," he said.

"No," I said and concentrated on his nail, but I could feel my crotch getting warm.

"Come on," he said. "I promise I'll keep totally still."

I rolled off him slightly and let him pull my panties over my hips, and then quickly got back on top of him so that the panties would bind my thighs, framing my ass for him to watch. I heard him suck his breath in. "Yeah, honey, that's really nice. Damn, you got a sweet ass."

I heard him pulling the pillows around so that he could sit up, and I moved back a little toward his hips. His fingers traced the line of panties on my thighs. He put his hands on my hips and pulled me farther back, toward him, so that I was sitting just below his pelvis. My hips started rolling unconsciously, and the tip of his dick nosed against my ass.

"Can you still reach, baby?" he said softly. "God, you're a pervert, you know that? I can't believe you want to do this to me."

He continued to run his fingertips over my hips and the small of my back as I prepared to paint the other nails. I started with the smallest toe this time, round like a little jelly bean, so that I could do his big toe last. The nail on the little toe was ridged and dry around the cuticle.

"Wait a sec," I said, and leaned all the way over for the oil on the nightstand. Mike held firmly onto my hips so that I had to stretch for it. With one hand, I flipped the cap open with my thumb and held the bottle a few inches over his foot. I squeezed the bottle and a thick stream of oil shot out, splashing onto the top of his foot, leaving drops on the bedsheets. I heard Mike gasp as the liquid pooled and ran into the furrows on his foot.

"Honey, that's nice," I purred, rubbing the oil on top of his foot, between his toes, all the way up to his toenails. I was careful not to get any on the nails themselves or the polish wouldn't set.

"Oh, yeah," he sighed. "Hurry up with that, would you? I've got things I need to do to you."

"Just wait. This isn't for you, this is for me. I'll let you know when I'm done."

Mike rocked his hips under mine, and I rolled my ass again for him as I took the brush from the bottle. My left hand was slippery from the oil, and I had to move slowly. The liquid looked like candy, like molten sugar. It shone on his nails with tiny, lilac-colored squares of light, reflected from the lamp on the table. Finally, I got to the big toe again. I dipped the brush three or four times, collecting rich drops of color on the surface of his nail, and then stroking the brush in the liquid until the whole nail was covered. The smell was overpowering, a thin, chemical odor. I flared my nostrils and took a really deep breath.

"Hey, when is this going to be done?" I didn't answer him. "Hey!" he said, louder, and slapped my ass again. I knew that would please him. "Oh, yeah," he grunted, grabbing my ass with both hands, pulling my buttocks apart. I raised my hips and rocked my clit sideways against his thigh as I leaned down and licked the divot behind his ankle.

"Damn, Claire," he groaned, slipping his thumb down to press against my clit. "What are you doing to me?"

"Nothing," I said, darting my tongue into the cleavage between his toes. Then I pulled back a little and blew gently on the wet spot my tongue had left. His feet twitched, and he pushed his other thumb into my pussy.

His nails, nearly dry now, had taken on an even, hard shine. The deep, manufactured color made him look nearly unreal, as though he were made of something other than flesh. I kneaded his ankles as he fucked me with his thumb, pressing his fingers against my ass. He slipped his other thumb in too, and opened me up. "Oh, Claire, baby, this is beautiful," he groaned. I pushed my hips farther back, and he bumped forward and got his dick up against my ass. It was hard, hot, and smooth.

I was still facing away from him. Mike took hold of my hips, picked me up, and then sat me down hard, too hard, on his cock. I gasped and leaned forward. I rested my hands on his knees. He was so hard that it hurt to have him so deep in me, but he was hanging onto my hips and forcing me to ride him. I kept watching his toes, concentrating on those ten grape candy moons, twitching as our bodies moved. His hands were warm and strong. His breathing got heavier.

He pulled his toes back and the sinews got very taut. The shadows in the furrows between them changed shape as his feet moved. He tried to raise his knees but I still had them pinned to the bed. It hurt to ride him so roughly, but watching the shadows moving, watching the polish shining in the dim light, made me feel as if this were mine, all mine.

His feet and toes jerked and tensed, curling, flexing when he came.

"Ahhhh," he said, for a long time. I carefully lifted myself off him. In the bathroom, I started the hot water, and then took a washcloth to him and cleaned his dick and balls. "Oh, thank you, baby," he murmured. He put his hand out to my cheek. His eyes were closed. I took his hand and kissed the palm, hard, smelling his fingers and covering my face with his hand. Smelled like a man. Like my man.

THE ALBUM

Kate Dominic

Kʀɪs ᴀɴᴅ I ᴋᴇᴇᴘ ᴀ sᴘᴇᴄɪᴀʟ ᴘʜᴏᴛᴏ ᴀʟʙᴜᴍ, one that's just the two of us together. No family, no friends, no professional accomplishments. Just us. Even the wedding pictures in there are strictly personal—me eating the cake from his fingers, him taking my garter off with his teeth, the two of us sleeping naked in each other's arms early the next morning. He actually got up and set the timer for that picture, cuddling back up against me just as the flash went off.

Over the years, we've made a habit of including everyday photos along with the special ones. It's our journal, though the album itself isn't particularly fancy—a plain leather binder with acid-free pages. Whole months can go by without our taking it down off the shelf. Other times, we keep it open on the dresser while we're deciding what to add next. But, like any good book, it opens to some pages automatically.

The photo of us at the biker bar is one of my favorites. "Melissa and Her Pet," the caption reads. Just two leather dykes, dressed to kill in black and silver, sitting at a table with the end of a leash barely visible in my hand. It was our fifth anniversary, and the waitress took the picture. Kris's drag was perfect. Not that it doesn't seem strange to call cowhide and chains "drag." But he was dressed to kill. The shot doesn't capture the smoky, sweaty ambiance of the bar. Not quite. But we'd met in a bar, and somehow that made the picture perfect.

We met in one of those dives down on Sunset Boulevard. Kris was fronting a gay punk band from D.C. that was opening for one of the local big names. I walked in the door with my actor friends. As my eyes adjusted to the darkness and my ears numbed to the assault from the speakers, I looked up into the glare of the stage lights—at the most gorgeous human being I'd ever seen. He was obviously a guy. He was dancing in his jockey shorts, and no fake parts ever moved the way his did when he thrust his hips forward. He wasn't hard, just hung.

His chest was very muscular, despite his slender build. I could see his nipple rings move beneath the glitter of his sleeveless Judy Garland T-shirt as he danced. It was his face that really drew me in, though. Kris was truly beautiful, in the classic artistic sense. Soft hazel eyes accented with a minimum of the black kohl outlining obligatory for a punk singer, vibrantly full lips, and delicate cheek bones framed by a cloud of straight blonde hair that just brushed the edges of his shoulders. A thickly studded leather slave collar covered his Adam's apple, and as he pranced around in his shiny combat boots, belting out one indecent song after another, his wicked smile sparkled in his eyes. I blushed when he bent over from the waist, knees locked straight and feet spread wider than his shoulders, and wiggled his ass up against the bassist. The other guy actually moved his guitar to one side so that Kris could rub against his crotch. It was obscene and sexy, and I was in lust with Kris from the moment he stood up, vigorously rubbed his crotch, and then looked at the audience in mock surprise as the front of his sweaty white jockeys swelled. Damn, that man is an exhibitionist!

Ed, one of the guys in our crowd, sputtered every time he looked at Kris. Now Ed is straight, straight, straight. But he kept shaking his head and saying, "I'm so glad I'm married! If that guy were in a dress, I'd chase his ass until I caught it! Damn, he's beautiful!" Then he'd shake his head and take another long swig of beer.

Cynthia, his wife and my former roommate, just cuffed him on the shoulder and laughed. It takes a lot to faze Cyn. After three beers she took Ed's car keys, and then we left the rest of our friends and went upstairs to sit down and watch the show. Cyn was thoroughly enjoying Ed's dilemma. She had her hand in his lap under the table but I could see her arm moving, and she had a really evil grin on her face. Every once in a while, Ed would close his eyes and groan, and Cyn would lean over and tongue his ear while she poured another drink down his throat. She kept telling him he was going to have sweet dreams that night. I figured he probably would if she kept that up.

They were so engrossed in each other I knew they wouldn't miss me if I found some action on my own, so I pretty much kept my eyes glued to the stage, and to Kris, for the rest of the set. Just watching him gave me a major case of the hots, which is frustrating as all hell when you know the guy is gay.

I almost didn't recognize him when I bumped into him, literally, a couple of hours later. The headlining band was setting up, and I didn't see Kris come up in back of me to lean against the balcony rail. I heard Ed groan, and when I looked at my buddy, his eyes were somewhere over my shoulder. Cyn just laughed, put her hand over his eyes, and pulled him down against her breasts.

"Drunk," she grinned up at the space in back of me.

I heard this really clear tenor laugh behind me. I turned around, bumping into a very solid thigh, and there was Kris. He looked different with clothes on. Same T-shirt, but pink spandex pants and a wide black leather belt. He'd shed most of the makeup, but damn, he was still gorgeous. It took me a second to get over my initial shock at seeing him up close. Then I managed to clear my throat and compliment him on his band's set.

"Cute song about the ice-cube blow jobs," I smiled.

"You heard us?" he asked excitedly. Kris is one of those people whose whole face comes alive when he talks. "There weren't that many people here when we played. I was afraid that'd affect the CD sales, but they're really moving."

Cyn nodded him toward the chair where Ed's feet were resting; Ed was passed out, so Kris carefully pushed his feet onto the floor and sat down. The headlining act was starting, and Kris pulled his chair right up next to me and leaned over so that we could talk, or at least try to, between songs. It was too loud to really hear, though. When it became obvious he was reading my lips, I raised my eyebrows at him and he just gave me this big grin and pulled back the edge of his hair. He'd put in earplugs. I grinned back and discreetly lifted my hair so that he could see I had, too. I think Cyn must have thought we were nuts with how hard we started laughing. It was right then that one of his band's publicity guys snapped a shot of us. It was supposed to have been a pic of Kris enjoying the rest of the show, but the photo didn't fit quite with the band's image, so the guy gave Kris the picture. It's the first one in our album. Kris called it "Fate."

After the show, he asked me out for coffee. We helped Cyn drag Ed to the car and waved them off. Then we walked down a couple of blocks to a little diner and split a piece of pecan pie. Three cups of coffee later, Kris shocked the hell out of me. He was telling me about how the band had started, when he stopped in mid-sentence. He leaned over and he kissed me, full on the lips. All I could do was stare at him, stunned.

Kris is straight.

I suppose I should qualify that a bit. Kris is at least as straight as I am. Neither one of us could claim to be a Kinsey 0. We're both young and horny, and we work in entertainment. But our same-sex flings had usually been one-nighters. Anyway, we spent the weekend together, getting to know each other. Yes, biblically as much as anything else. As I said, we were young and horny, and there's a whole lot of chemistry between us.

On Monday he flew back to D.C., and we started a long-distance romance. His band toured up and down the East Coast, and I landed a series of walk-ons as well as a few commercials, enough to pay the bills. Especially my phone bills, which by the fall were getting pretty impressive, even at night rates.

The band came back out a couple of times over the next eight months. By then, Kris and I were getting serious. That April we discovered that neither one of us had been sleeping with anyone else since we'd met. It's quite a shock to find out you've fallen in love with someone without even realizing it. That night he asked me to marry him. How old-fashioned, huh? And I said yes.

That summer the band moved out to L.A., and in August, a year after we met, Kris and I got married. Ed and Cyn stood up for us.

I have to admit, I'd never realized how much I'd like being married. We're both vegetarians and we can both cook, which probably kept us from starving that first year. But I really think I could have lived on the sex alone. We'd both tested negative, so I went on the pill, and we went crazy with a general frenzy of uninhibited fucking. We discovered we both loved missionary, and we spent hours with his hair and sweat falling down onto my face as he glided into me. There were times we went at it until we were so sore that the only thing that could soothe us was the thick, slippery cream of our orgasms.

We're also supportive of each other's careers. Having two performers in the same family can be a real downfall for a lot of couples. We stuck it out, and during our second year we both started working more regularly, which helped a lot financially. But we also started spending less time in bed together, and more time sleeping when we were there. The sex was still good—comforting and fulfilling—and to this day, just thinking of Kris lying in bed with a hard-on is enough to make me wet. But some of the excitement was gone, along with the frequency, and every once in a while I missed the frantic edge we used to have.

I hadn't realized that Kris was missing it too. It took us a while to figure out that communication is something you have to work at in a marriage. But I remember to the minute when we started talking about our sex life. It was just after our second anniversary, the day Kris called up, out of the blue, to ask me to lunch. I'd taken a temp job as an administrative assistant at a recording studio so that we'd have some extra money for vacation, and he'd been working down the street that morning. At noon, the receptionist called to say Kris was waiting for me in the lobby, and I walked up front to meet him.

I'd gone all the way into the room before I realized the person standing in front of me was my husband. Then, it was a good thing I was too stunned to move, because otherwise I probably would have fallen over from the shock. If I hadn't seen him with scarves tied around his neck so many times before on stage, I'd never have recognized him. Or should I say "her." Kris was wearing a demure Laura Ashley floral print sundress, matching espadrilles, and a stylishly floppy straw hat with a large pink ribbon that complemented the scarf tied loosely around his neck. His, or rather her, hair was impeccably styled, a froth of carefree waves through which she brushed her carefully manicured nails. In short, she was beautiful. And as she winked seductively, each and every one of those lechers I was working with gave her an appreciative once-over as they walked out the door to lunch.

Before I could collect myself enough to say anything, Kris swooped over and embraced me like a long-lost friend, carefully bussing my cheek so as not to mess up her makeup as she whispered in my ear, "Your girlfriend has the hots for you, babe. Play your part. I've got us a hotel room a couple of blocks away."

Linking her arm in mine, Kris turned us toward the door. "Thanks, Jenna honey. You're such a doll."

"Glad to help, Krissie." As usual, the vacuous young lady gracing the receptionist's desk giggled as she spoke. "I think it's so neat when roommates stay in touch. Imagine, after three whole years, you only have one day in town."

Krissie hugged her breast to my arm. "You sure you don't mind covering for Melissa for a couple of hours? We have so much to catch up on."

"Oh, no problem," Jenna replied. "Everybody will be tied up at that finance meeting the rest of the afternoon anyway. Just have her back by four and they'll never know she was missing."

Jenna twittered, and then blushed with pleasure as Krissie handed her a disposable "tourist" camera to take a couple of quick pictures of the two "roommates" together.

As we walked out into the sunlight, Krissie didn't give me much chance to talk. She linked her arm in mine, pressed her bosom against me, and kept up a running, steamy commentary about how nice it was to be back in L.A. where "grrrls" didn't have to worry about having their afternoons interrupted. Most of what she was saying was lost in the whir of the noon traffic, so I just let her lead me down the sidewalk, the light scent of her perfume tickling my nose. Ten minutes later, she swept me into a reasonably nice hotel room where there was a bucket of Chardonnay chilling on the nightstand, the covers were turned back on a queen-sized bed, and the sun streamed in through the gauze privacy curtains of a fifth-story picture window.

I'd gotten over my initial shock, so I turned to my erstwhile roommate and said, "To what do I owe the honor of your visit, Krissie?"

Kris came up to me and gently drew the tip of his finger over my cheek and down the side of my face. "We're getting too complacent, Liss," he said quietly. His fingers were soft and silky as he stroked further along the edge of my neck, making me shiver. "We're too good for that." The finger dropped lower, tracing the outline of my breast, and then rubbing slow circles over the nipple. "I want to see the sparkle back in your eyes when I touch you." I could feel my skin reach for him, and he smiled as the tip hardened under his touch.

"Now I'm your girlfriend, Krissie, your former roommate who's back in town just for one day, and I want a slow afternoon of the kind of girl-to-girl sex you used to have." As Krissie spoke, she started softly milking my breasts with her enamel-tipped fingers. "I want to get lipstick on your nipples and lick your clit, maybe even make you come all over my face the way you do when I press your G-spot just right with a nice, thick dildo. I brought a couple with me, you know.

"When I'm done I'm going to give you my pussy to play with, Liss. Maybe if I'm really lucky, you'll suck my girly clit. You've never seemed to mind that it's bigger than most grrrls'." She sucked softly on my lower lip as I finally smiled. "What do you say, love?"

I could feel Krissie's "clit" pressing against my leg, and all of a sudden, even though I knew it was Kris—I mean, I really knew that the whole time we were there—suddenly he was Krissie. I was kissing another woman in a way I hadn't for a long, long time, and I wanted her. My pussy was sopping wet and I wanted grrrl sex like you wouldn't believe.

"Krissie," I moaned, just her name, and I melted into her arms. Then we were kissing, the kind of soft, wet, tasting kisses that usually only two women can share. I took her hat off and buried my face in her neck so that her perfume made even her sweat seem feminine. Salty and sexy and so very, very sweet.

Every giggle was part of the foreplay. Krissie stripped me naked and then stood me in front of the mirror so that I could watch her playing with my body. She left pink circles of lipstick around my aureolas when she suckled me, her soft hands playing my pussy with her carefully manicured fingertips.

When I tried to touch her in return, she shook her head and touched her sticky fingers to my lips. "This first one's for you, sweetheart," she murmured, shivering slightly as I licked. "Just let me make you feel good."

So I did. I lay down on the bed with my legs spread, and Krissie got between them. The soft cotton of her dress brushed against my naked thigh as she nuzzled my breasts, licking and sucking and teasing. When my skin was so sensitized I could hardly stand it any more, she kissed her way down my belly. Then she settled herself between my legs, took my hips in her hands, and lifted me to her lips. It was Kris's strength, yet now somehow it was feminine, as she slowly kissed my labia as if she was making love to my mouth. First the outer lips and then the inner ones. And when she reached my clit, she played it as if it was my tongue. With infinite patience, she stroked and sucked and nibbled as if we were kissing. My whole body relaxed, and slowly, tenderly, Krissie's wonderful, loving mouth drew a climax from deep in the pit of my belly. She laughed, her tongue working constantly as I thrashed beneath her, screaming out my pleasure. When I finally collapsed onto the bed, she lapped the cream of my orgasm off me with her suddenly sandpapery tongue.

When I recovered enough to move, Krissie finally let me undress her. I drew away each piece of her clothing slowly, revealing my lover's body bit by bit. Except for a small triangle above her crotch, she'd shaved her whole body. Everywhere, her skin smelled and tasted of silky-soft peaches.

Krissie insisted I leave her underwear on, though she finally acquiesced to my taking her bra off when I told her how much I wanted to suck on her nipple rings. I reassured her that several of my female lovers had been small-breasted, so she didn't need to be self-conscious. Then I took her nipples, first one, then the other, into my mouth and worked them until she was moaning.

Although she insisted on keeping her panties on, plus her garter belt and stockings, I untied the ribbons that held the slit crotch of her panties closed, and then worked my lips over her thoroughly engorged and extremely large clit. It didn't take long at all for Krissie to come. She shook in my arms as I sucked her with the same tender intensity she'd given to me.

When she'd recovered, Krissie got out a couple of curved dildos, and we lay side-by-side and brought each other to "G-spot" orgasms that left the sheets soaked. Sated, we curled up and napped, and when I awoke, Krissie was finger-fucking me, not quite fisting me, but almost. I was so hungry for her that I came all over her hand. Again.

At home that night, we started talking, and, well, we learned to talk about sex. Not just idle talk, but real communication. We talked about our fantasies, both the things we wanted to do and the things that were best left in our heads. And we've kept on talking—and doing—ever since. We're performers, and, I admit, we're sort of exhibitionists. And we like variety. So we've acted out a lot of our fantasies. We've been girlfriends and boyfriends. We've traded genders. We've done bondage and S/M in exotic scenarios. But it's always been just the two of us. When we're brutally honest with each other, we need and want the security of monogamy. We want to be all the people the other one needs sexually. Luckily, we're good enough thespians that we've been able to pull it off. So far, at least.

I'd be lying if I said it was all easy. Mostly it has been; but the most difficult time for us was pretty much the year we both turned 30. Some people call it the "seven-year itch." All I know is that Kris suddenly got so hungry for man-sex that for the first time, we were afraid for our relationship.

On the night he came home shaken because he'd almost picked up some guy after a show, I figured I only had one card left to play. Now I'm not a man and I've never wanted to be, though I've played one—successfully—on stage. Usually it's Kris who does the drag. But all I could think of was the day Krissie came to visit me at work. She'd been there for me. So I cut my hair really short, changed my clothes, and threw myself into a new character as if I was playing for my life.

That's how we ended up in a gay leather bar near Modesto one night about a week later, me with a slave collar on and Kris in a particularly nasty mood. We'd ridden into town on Ed's Harley, and after a quick stop to get a hotel room, we headed out for the evening. You can see the look on Kris's face in the snapshot the woman at the front desk took of us as we left on the bike. He was feeling mean and toppish, and he was treating me the way he would some trick he'd picked up in an alley.

We were both wearing leather pants and jackets and our old but well-shined black boots, the ones we wear when we're doing heavy S/M. This time, though, beneath the jacket Kris was bare-chested except for a leather-and-nickel harness that gleamed like his nipple rings, and he had a diamond stud in his left ear. His hair was clubbed back with a leather bootlace, and he hadn't been near a razor for three days, so his face seemed dirty as well as unshaven. As I said, Kris looked mean, and I looked pissed. It's an unusual picture for us. Normally, we're smiling. But not that time. I'd become my husband's untrained little slave boy and was wearing the other earring in my right ear, just above where the leash clamped to the D-ring in my collar.

It was late when we got to the bar. Most everybody else there was at least half-drunk. As part of our characters, we looked pretty wasted too, though Kris had only been sipping at his bourbon and I'd just spilled some beer on my T-shirt to get the smell rising. I didn't want to get the shirt too wet, because even though I'd bound my breasts, they'd still be noticeable if my nipples got too hard.

We were at a table in a dark corner, and I was starting to get more than a little annoyed at how often Kris was yanking on my leash. The room was crowded and, except for the occasional tug, he was ignoring me, trading crude comments with a group of guys around the table. I was getting even more uncomfortable from the rather sizable butt plug he'd shoved up my ass when we first got to the hotel. He'd said he wanted his boy ready for him, and by midnight the "boy" was real convinced that the plug had stretched his anal muscles wide enough for a truck to drive through. The leather pants held the plug in tightly, and I was horny from squirming against it. Especially after the vibration of the bike ride.

Suddenly, Kris reached up and grabbed a handful of my hair, at least as much as he could of it, and shoved my face down hard against the wet, beer-covered table.

"What the fuck?!" I snapped, barely remembering to keep my voice low.

He yanked viciously on my hair. It didn't really hurt—it was more for show—but it startled me and I yelped. He'd never treated me like that before. He leaned over and growled in my ear, "You need some training, boy. I want your ass, and I want it now!"

I couldn't believe what I was hearing. I felt his hand on my hip, and then the slow slide of the zipper moving down the back of my leather pants. I panicked. Shit, we were in a gay leather bar way to hell-and-gone in the middle of nowhere, and those guys would have killed us if they'd found out I was a chick. I was struggling against Kris when suddenly, I felt a strange pair of hands grab my forearms and slam me down against the table.

"Stop fightin', boy!" the voice snapped. "Your daddy wants your ass, he *gets* it!"

"Bullshit!" I yelled back, my voice higher than it should have been, but no one seemed to notice.

I jumped and gasped as Kris slapped me hard across the ass. Then the cool air kissed my crack and asshole as the zipper came down the rest of the way, and, mortified, I froze as Kris yanked the butt plug out of my ass. I mean, right there in front of all those people he pulled that plug out and dumped it into his drink! The other guy was laughing so hard the table was shaking, and his friends crowded around to make sure no one would disturb us.

Then I heard the quick tear of a condom wrapper, and the next thing I knew, Kris was bending over me, his weight pressing me hard into the edge of the table, and his thick, hot cock slid up my ass. Right there in the bar, with a good dozen people watching us, he was fucking me over a dirty, wet table.

Now Kris knows how much I like having sex in public, when we act as if we're alone but we really know people are watching us. But this was way beyond anything I'd bargained for. Fortunately, my ass was so loose that he slid right in. The others may have thought it was a rough fuck, but he used that butt plug specifically because it was just the right size to get me ready for his cock. And he'd stuffed half a tube of lube up me when he'd put the plug in, so I was slick inside. I still struggled, though. The other guy was holding me down, and I was just mad enough that it felt good to fight, especially since by then I was pretty sure the other guy was strong enough to keep me from getting away.

It was odd. I'd never had any rape fantasies. I sure as hell never wanted to be raped in reality. But suddenly, being held helpless while Kris pounded into me brought out a wildness I'd never felt before. I was scared to death those guys would discover I was a chick, and yet all I could think about was how hot it was for Kris to be fucking me in front of all those people. I climaxed from the anal stimulation alone. It was rough and fast, and when Kris was done he just pulled out, stuffed the icy plug back up my ass, and zipped my pants closed again.

I was still gasping when the other guy let go of me and Kris dragged my head up off the table, kissing me so hard his teeth drew blood. I could taste the copper on my lips as he said, "Your ass is mine again, boy, as soon as we get back to the hotel. Now move it!"

The people standing around were still laughing as Kris tossed a twenty on the table for a round of beer. Then he dragged me out the door, threw me on the bike, and took me back to our room.

It was the most violent night we've ever spent together, and it turned me on incredibly: I knew, at a very fundamental level, that all I had to do was say "stop" and he would.

But I didn't say it. I stayed in character. I argued with him and mouthed off, telling him I'd never submit to him. I wasn't the least bit surprised when he stuffed my shirt in my mouth, threw me over the end of the bed, and whipped my bare ass with his belt until I was screaming. I knew I'd have bruises. It hurt like hell, and he was swinging the belt full out, with the buckle wrapped around his fist and the strap burning into my ass cheeks. But I wouldn't say "stop." I'd never played the part of an untrained biker boy before, of Kris's boy, and I wanted to do it. When he fucked me again, this time without a rubber, he put me on all fours, doggy style, so that he was banging against my sore ass with each stroke. Then he reached around and pulled on my clit, "jacking off my little slave-boy cock," he called it. And he waited to come until he felt my orgasm shudder through my body.

I cried myself to sleep on his shoulder. My ass hurt, but that wasn't why I was crying. It was just so intense. So raw and violent. We'd brought out parts of ourselves we'd never let each other see before. When I brushed my hand across Kris's cheek, I felt tears running down into his hair. We clung to each other with the strength of those who have fought a war together and won, but now had to live with the knowledge of the demons that lived inside us.

The next morning, our actual anniversary, I fucked Kris with a strap-on. I woke up to find him spooned in front of me, pressing his ass back against me in his sleep. I cuddled against him for a while, listening to the soft purr of his snoring. Then I carefully disentangled myself, slipped out of bed, and got out the harness. I hadn't told him I'd brought it. I just put it on, along with my leather jacket and a motorcycle cap, and splashed on some of the male cologne I'd been wearing on the trip. Then I climbed back into bed, pulled Kris's top leg up toward his chest, and started playing with his asshole.

It didn't take long before he was moaning in his sleep. He was relaxed and loose as I stretched him, stuffing lube up his butt. He didn't wake up until the head of the dildo slipped into him, but then he woke up fast.

"What the fuck?" he grumbled, trying to lower his leg. He stopped only when he felt my fingernails digging into his thigh.

"I'm fucking you, boy," I said, low and mean. I slid my hand over his hip, slapping him sharply when he jumped as I slid further into him. "You're my little pussy-boy this morning."

"Dammit, Lissa! How big is that thing? It's splitting me in two!" Kris can be grumpy in the morning, and he was tense as a bowstring. But my butt was still sore from the night before, so even though I stopped moving, I was in no mood to back out.

"Shut up and hold still," I growled. It was hard keeping my voice that low, but I felt I needed to stay in character. "If you fight, it's going to hurt. And I don't want to hurt you. But I *am* going to fuck you. I'm going to fuck your tight little ass until you shoot all over the bed. So relax, boy." On the word "relax," I pushed in a tiny bit further, hearing him hiss.

Finally, I felt his hips give, and he moaned into the pillow. Then his shoulders twitched as his whole body untightened and he shook his head, laughing softly, "Whatever you say, sir. But may I please roll over and stick my ass in the air so I'm at the right angle to take your hard, hot cock? Sir?"

"OK, boy," I said gruffly, trying to keep from smiling as I slapped his ass again. I let go of his leg, but I didn't pull out. I made him roll over with me in him, and I didn't back up when he lifted his pelvis to put a pillow underneath, just listened to him grunt as the fake dick slid in a little bit further. To tell you the truth, I didn't want him to see how big that latex cock was. If he'd had any idea what I was fucking him with, he would have pitched a fit.

When he was in position, I made him rest his head on his folded arms. "You can drop down and rub your cock against the pillow if you want, but you can't touch it," I said. Then I straddled his legs and pressed a little bit further into him.

I pressed further, and further, leaning onto his back as I moved forward. Sometimes I'd pull back and fuck in and out a few times, to keep him really loose. And on each stroke I'd go in a little bit further. But I still hadn't bottomed out.

That dildo was huge. It was ten inches long and two inches wide, and I slid it damn near all the way up his ass.

"Jeez, Lissa. I can feel that thing almost to my throat," he whispered, grinding his hips against me. Then he got really still, and I suddenly realized he was looking in the mirror by the side of the bed.

"You want to watch your ass getting fucked, boy?" I asked quietly, knowing he was going to watch one way or the other. So I slowly and deliberately started backing out of him, not all the way, just until only the head was in him. I could see his eyes getting wider as he watched the monster pull out, and then his whole body stiffened as I slowly started pressing back in again.

"Jesus, Lissa! That's too big! Really, I mean it! Stop!" He gasped and tightened hard beneath me.

I froze. He'd said stop and I did, in mid-stroke. But I didn't pull out. Instead, I rested my weight fully onto my legs and massaged his shoulders. "Relax, boy," I said, calmly, still staying in character and hoping he'd be able to drop back into the scene. "It's not too big. You've already had it in you.

"Come on, boy. You want to be fucked. You need to be fucked." I traced my fingers up his spine and smiled as I felt him shudder. "Relax and let me give you what you need. You know I'll stop if you really can't take it."

For the longest time he just lay there, looking at the dildo in the mirror. Tension gradually drained out of his shoulders. I dragged my hand down his back and caressed his lower butt cheeks, where his thighs met his lower curves.

"Give me your ass, boy. You know how much I want it. And I'll make you feel real good." I carefully massaged the tautly stretched skin surrounding the dildo, gently relaxing and stretching him. "Tell me you want it, boy. Tell me so I can fuck you. So I can press your hot come right up out of your ass."

A very long minute later, Kris relaxed underneath me. Then he looked back over his shoulder and laughed shakily. "OK, sir. But will you kiss me, so I'm not so afraid?"

"Of course I will, boy." I bent over, opening my mouth, and gave him my tongue to suck on. Then I slowly started pressing into him again. He moaned softly as I slid further down. When my weight was resting full on him and I was deep in his ass, he whispered, "Please, sir. Please fuck your boy." I gave him one more deep, passionate kiss, and then I leaned back up, grabbed his hips, and started fucking him hard—long, sure, deliberate strokes. He whimpered and twitched beneath me. Then, on one stroke, I moved just a bit differently, pushing down toward the front of his belly just a bit more, and suddenly he arched up and gasped as if he couldn't get enough air into his lungs. I froze.

"That hurt, boy?" I asked, holding myself motionless.

"No, sir!" He gasped. "Please, sir. Please," His whole body was shuddering as if he was suddenly very cold or scared. Then with a long, low moan, he dropped his head back on his arms and whispered. "Please, sir. Do it again."

"Yeah," I grinned. I arched into him, a long, slow glide that made him moan with pleasure, and then I pulled back. And when I slid in again, Kris let out a high, keening cry and his whole body shook as I pressed down hard into him. I didn't think he'd ever stop coming as that hard latex dick pressed cum-loads of his semen right straight out of his prostate. The vibration of his body was almost enough to make me come. And still he kept shuddering.

When his body collapsed onto his arms, I pulled out. I took off the harness, lay down on the bed, and ordered him onto all fours over me. His arms and legs were still shivering as I took his soft, sticky cock in my mouth and let it rest there, tonguing it gently while I slid my fingers in and out of his loose, well-fucked asshole. Then I told him to suck my hard man-cock until I came.

"Yes, sir," he whispered, groaning against my hands as he took my comparatively tiny clit-cock into his mouth. But he sucked and played it for all he was worth, like a good little slave boy. It took me about two heartbeats to come all over his face and, without being told, he dutifully licked the cream from my pussy. When he finally turned around and collapsed into my arms, we both started laughing. We laughed until tears streamed down our faces.

"Damn, Lissa," he choked out, shaking his head as he pulled the dildo from the harness and looked at it. "What the hell ever made you think you could get that up my ass?"

I shrugged. "You said you needed to be man-fucked, and this was as 'manly' as I could get!"

Then we were both laughing again. Before we left the hotel, we had the manager take another picture of us on the bike. The album captions say, "Before, and After." And we didn't make a journal entry to go with that trip. We're the only ones who need to know the details. Beyond that, the looks on our faces say it all.

This last picture, "Ten Years," is the one the concierge took of us as we were leaving for the opera in San Francisco last weekend. We decided to reverse genders that night, so Kris wore a glittering strapless gold lamé ball gown with a *faux* fur stole and the most realistic-looking costume pearls I've ever seen. He was stunning. I wore a black tux and, as the picture shows, I've finally mastered makeup to show just a hint of a five o'clock shadow.

The performance was wonderful. We didn't even try to talk, just sat there quietly holding hands while the music flowed over us. When we got back to the hotel room, I fucked him with the strap-on while I fingered his enormous clit until he shot all over the bed. And he gave my little clitty-cock the most wonderful blow job, licking and sucking in all the right places while he wiggled a finger up my ass. I came like gangbusters.

But this morning, this precise morning, it's been exactly one decade since we first promised ourselves to each other. So we celebrated like any other long-time married couple. We had breakfast at home in our own bed. We took a long, slow, sexy shower together. And then Kris climbed on top of me, plain old missionary position, his biceps flexing over me as he took his weight on his arms while he glided in and out, in and out, with all the timing we've learned so well over the years. When I couldn't hold back any more, when I cried out as my orgasm washed over me, I felt the deep, swelling thrust as Kris surged into me, his semen bathing my cervix—so deeply, profoundly satisfying. And so hot that my body curled around him.

As I dozed off, I could feel myself smiling against his lips. This time, we didn't take a photograph. But over the years I've learned to know Kris pretty well: I have no doubt I'll see a flash in my sleep sometime before tomorrow morning.

CYCLES

Jean Roberta

"ARE YOU USING BOTH MACHINES?"

The voice managed to combine a certain well-bred politeness with a hint of desperation. I was in the laundry room, bending over the dryer, so I couldn't see him at all. I was sure he was getting a clear view of me.

I straightened up fast. "Yes," I said, willing myself not to feel embarrassed—I didn't want to tell my fellow tenant that nearly every machine in the entire apartment complex was filled with my clothing. That's how I do it when I have a lot of laundry. I figure this is actually more considerate than using the machines in my own building for long periods.

"Will you be finished soon?" he persisted. He was trying to control a grin, but his dark, piercing eyes were disconcerting. They were set in a face with prominent cheekbones, a chiseled nose, and full, sensuous lips. He seemed to be in his thirties. He was of average height, but his slim body and graceful stance suggested an unusual occupation: dance, theater, fitness, perhaps martial arts.

"Do you need to wash something right away?" I heard myself asking. *Why offer this man favors?* howled the voice of my self-respect.

"Well, yes." He flashed me a smile, intended to be charming. "I need to wash this." He shook out a silk turquoise evening gown with a 1920s-style dropped waist and a handkerchief hem. "It's washable," he explained, as if we were friends, "though I'm not sure I can get the stain out of the skirt." I did not want to know the origin of the stain.

He obviously wanted a reaction from me, and I wanted to maintain my cool at all costs. I ignored his need for advice on removing stains; I was hardly an expert on the subject. "You can put it in before I do my next load," I told him.

My reckless phrase brought the tickled grin back to his face. "Thank you," he intoned deeply, like a lion purring. He seemed to be suggesting thanks for something I hadn't offered. "I'm Serge, by the way, in 3-D."

I resisted the urge to make a smart crack about his apartment number. "I'm Sherry," I answered, not wanting him to know more about me than that.

Luckily, I had to turn away from him to pull my laundry out of the washer and stuff it into the dryer. I felt his eyes on my behind as if they were hands.

"Sherry," he said, tasting my name on his tongue. "Foyer, I think it is, though you use the pen name Palabra, at least for some of your writing. Do you want to keep that identity separate from your role as a librarian?"

His words jolted through my guts like an electric shock. I faced him, showing my anger. "How..." I began, but he interrupted me.

"Do you feel threatened?" he asked gently. His eyes looked unbearably sympathetic. "I didn't mean to invade your privacy. I came across some of that information by accident. But after all, you can't expect your life to be a secret once you've been published. As a certain critic once said, anyone who's published a book is standing around in public with their pants down, waiting to see what will happen."

This felt like the last slap, in some sense, especially from a man who had a taste for women's clothing, who probably looked more convincing in it than I did, and who clearly enjoyed goading me—though he probably had no interest in getting my pants off for any reason I wanted to think about. But I *was* thinking about it. Damn my hyperactive imagination.

"Well, *I'm* not standing around," I retorted, wanting to get away. "I have other things to do."

"Sherry," he tempted, "won't you come to my place for a drink, just until our clothes are ready to come out?" It was my turn to grin at an unintended double-entendre. "I've been horribly rude, and I'd like to make it up to you. It's my Good Neighbor policy."

My curiosity wouldn't let me resist the bait. "OK," I said, accepting. "Just for a minute."

His apartment was tastefully furnished, mostly in pale woods, cream-colored fabrics, and reflecting surfaces that appealed to vanity and gave an illusion of space. I liked the way my short reddish-gold (or sherry-colored) hair framed my lightly freckled face and gray-green eyes in his hallway mirror, as if he'd invited me in because my color scheme complemented his. I also liked the way my faded T-shirt and paint-splattered jeans clashed with his decor, like graffiti on the walls of a trendy boutique.

"What would you like?" Serge asked. "Beer—domestic or imported—wine, scotch?" I was glad he had the good sense not to offer me a glass of sherry.

I asked for a beer from the local brewery. "I don't need a glass," I added. Seated on his sofa, I waited to be served. When he placed the bottle on a coaster on the coffee table in front of me, I jumped up to admire the view from his picture window. He was making me nervous.

"Are you running away from me, Sherry?" he needled. He approached me so quietly from behind that his hands on my shoulders were a surprise. I could smell his cologne and the clean scent of his skin underneath. Nothing about him was careless or masculine, in the style of the football-playing men of my youth. I felt like an animal, maybe a raccoon, that he'd discovered washing something in the local stream and had lured to his home with food, to see if the creature could be domesticated.

From my shoulders, his hands moved up to the edge of my neck, where he began massaging tension out of my muscles. I couldn't stand it. "Don't you prefer men?" I demanded.

He laughed as though I'd told a witty joke. "Sometimes," he admitted. "It depends who it is. I don't understand why people think plumbing is everything, do you? Human beings have so much else to offer. And besides, I spend most of my time working with women's bodies, deciding what would cover them best." His hands suddenly tightened on my upper back. "Oh, is that why you thought I was a queen? Because I'm a designer and dressmaker?"

I felt myself turning hot. I didn't want to admit that I'd thought he was washing one of his own favorite dresses.

He guessed. "Oh, you thought I was going to wear the silk...!" He chuckled. "It doesn't fit me, honey. I made it for someone else. I can show you the clothes I wear, and the ones I make for other people, so you can see the difference. When I design for my customers, I'm guided by their taste, not mine."

Don't tell me what I should wear, I thought, *especially on my weekends at home.* "OK," I said aloud, as though taking up a

dare. "Show me your work, and show me through your place."
I was terrified that if he didn't stop touching me soon, I wouldn't
be able to resist any other offers he might make.

"Fair enough," he agreed, tugging me gently by the arm.
"I've read your work, but you haven't seen mine. Or you didn't
know it."

He pulled me into a bedroom that was as seductive as I
expected; the *pièce de résistance* was a canopied bed piled high
with pillows and matching comforter. I couldn't help admiring
the round, muscular cheeks in my host's tight pants as he strode
to the closet, where he rummaged briskly through the contents
until he found what he was looking for. When he turned around
with a red beaded gown in his arms, he looked uncannily like a
grieving madonna holding the bloodstained body of her son.
He placed it carefully on the bed so that I could see it whole. "I
made this," he explained simply, "for him."

Serge glanced at a framed photo on the wall near the carved
oak bureau. It showed him with a shorter, younger man who
had curly black hair and a devilish grin. Both men were wearing
jeans and shirts in macho shades of putty and navy blue, but
with a certain ironic self-consciousness. Despite their arch
expressions, they looked so innocent that at first I hardly recognized the man in the picture as the one standing beside me.

"He used to perform," Serge explained, obviously struggling
to control his voice, an effort that made him uncharacteristi-
cally terse. "The gown," he paused and sighed, "goes with a
fake ruby necklace and earrings. They went to his sister after he
died." Serge's eyes shone with the dark brightness of a very
deep well.

I felt feverishly hot, and then icy cold. I was appalled to the
bone by this man's unwanted revelations: first the low comedy
of a transvestite relationship, then the shock, grief, and survivor
guilt of losing a fairly young lover, probably to a sexually trans-
mitted disease that had stolen him away like a successful rival. I

wanted to scream, "What do you want me to say? Why did you burden me with this?"

"Dick," he told me, as though I had asked. "That was his name. Actually, Diego. Five years ago."

I couldn't look at Serge. "I'm sorry," I murmured, falling back on convention. I wasn't willing to hug him, and his strong, silent expectation of physical comfort made me furious. I didn't want to admit to myself why hugging him would feel dangerous.

I backed out of the bedroom, his cave of memory. "I'm sorry," I repeated, "but you don't know me very well, and I don't think it was appropriate for you to tell me this." If I sounded like a cold bitch, I thought, so be it. "You invited me in for a drink. That was all. I think I should go check on my wash now."

Serge opened his arms toward me as if expecting me to walk into them. "I feel as if I know you, Sherry," he said, defending himself, "because I've read some of your stories. 'Survival' moved me. You understand grief too. Your life isn't a secret, you know. I think we both have things to offer each other." He waited for me to answer, but none of the words in my head seemed suitable, and hard experience had told me that words, once thrown into the air, can never be taken back. "Your laundry can wait," he urged gently.

"No, it can't," I insisted. "Almost every machine in this complex is full of my clothes, and they must all be ready by now. If I don't take them out soon, the Tenants' Committee will have an emergency meeting and put me through the spin cycle."

The change in his expression was like a sudden burst of sunlight. Opening his mouth as if to taste something delicious, he let out a guffaw that sounded much too hearty to go with his usual style. "Sherry, you are too much!" he howled, slapping one of my shoulders before I could stop him. "OK, then, let's go." I hadn't invited him to come along, but I couldn't stop him.

He followed behind me like a shadow, and his unseen presence at my back felt somehow threatening and comforting at the same time. I sped up, and we scampered briskly down the stairs to the basement laundry room. We probably looked like a comic dance team to the other tenants who passed by, but no one seemed interested in us.

I rushed to the washing machine, planning to pull out my clothes as quickly as possible. As soon as I bent over, though, Serge did something so crude that I felt light-headed: he pressed his crotch against my denim-covered bottom and wrapped his arms around my waist. "Sherry," he chuckled calmly, leaning toward my ears, "you know I want you."

Lust flooded through me like another surge of alcohol in my veins. My feelings were no subtler than his, but they were certainly complicated. The hardness of his cock through his pants spoke directly to the wetness in mine; what had he said about the irrelevance of sexual plumbing? He was male and I wanted him, or did I want him *because* he was male? But I also wanted him because he was feminine, with everything that that involved: charm, sensitivity, an eye for detail, a sweet smell, a certain body language. My heart ached for those qualities when I couldn't find them in another person. And yet I knew he was tempted to fuck me like an animal in this gathering place, a modern city version of a stream bank.

"Serge…" I began. I had no idea what to say, but I wasn't willing to surrender without conditions.

He pulled me up and turned me around as if leading me in a dance. With an urgency that was almost scary, he pulled me close and nuzzled my hair. "Just for now, honey," he assured me. "One minute at a time—that's all I'm asking." He kissed my throat in such a way that I could feel it in the soles of my feet. I moaned, and that was my answer.

"Serge," I said again. I twisted halfway out of his arms, making him laugh; he knew now that I wasn't rejecting him.

"Let's get your clothes." Like a helpful brother, he waited for me to reach into the washing machine and pull out armfuls of damp cloth. After taking them from me, he loaded them into the dryer. Our task was completed with impressive speed.

As soon as I turned away from him, he slapped my behind with such relish that I knew he'd wanted to do this from the moment he first saw me bent over the washing machine. The slap seemed to be a comment on my torn and stained jeans as well as on the cheeks they covered. Instead of making me angry, the slap made me feel weak in the knees, as echoes of the warm sting flooded through my guts and teased my pussy. For a moment, I couldn't move. "No, you won't get it again," he chuckled with a hand on my waist, "unless you hurry up."

At that moment I decided to suspend caution, good sense, and possibly even my self-respect. I'd been hungry for human touch for a year, since the abrupt departure of my last lover. I had been in shock for at least three months after the door slammed, and after that I'd plunged into solitary activities—especially writing—like a diver searching for treasure at the bottom of the ocean. No one could come between me and my muse, I thought, since she seemed more reliable than any fickle human companion.

Now I was faced with my hunger, and I had to admit that I was ready for what Serge was offering. Of course it would mess up my sense of identity and the image my friends seemed to have of me. That was actually part of the lure, like the call of my imagination: what hidden part of me would Serge summon forth, and vice versa? I was willing to find out.

We raced from building to building, and in each one we pulled wet clothes from a washing machine and stuffed them into a dryer, or pulled warm clothes from a dryer and folded them. Almost my entire wardrobe was in the machines, because I hadn't done any laundry while working on the last chapter of my novel. I had an image of all my clothes catching fire in the dryers, leaving me with nothing but what I was wearing. I wondered if Serge would design me a new wardrobe in that case, and if he'd find it amusing to keep me in his apartment naked (or clad in the lingerie of his choice) until he was finished.

He kept a hand on the back of my waist as we walked to the stairs leading to his apartment, and as we climbed them, his hand slid down to one of my cheeks where he could feel my muscles moving. I couldn't help wondering if he had usually done this with his male lovers, yet he seemed to appreciate my ass for its own qualities, and I was sure it didn't feel like a man's behind. I also suspected that he would enjoy discovering the rest of me in due course.

Somehow his apartment looked different when I visited it the second time, probably because I was entering with different expectations. Every piece of furniture now seemed to offer a different sexual experience: the carpet invited me to lie down on it and pull him down with me, the cream-colored sofa seemed to need some human fluids to spice up its blandness, and the matching chair looked like a suitable place for its owner to sit with an alert cock, waiting for me to ease myself onto it. But the bedroom was obviously where we were headed, and I was glad. I silently promised the living room I would get to know it better before long.

Of course Serge wanted to undress me first. He gently pulled the ends of my T-shirt out of my jeans, and I pulled it over my head and threw it aside as if I would never need it again. He smiled. He was looking at my old gray bra, and a blush spread over my face. He unhooked my bra in back with one smooth move, and it fell off my breasts like flotsam falling off a Venus rising from the waves. I thought I heard him sigh "ahh" as my nipples tightened and hardened under his gaze.

I was tingling from head to foot as he helped me pull my jeans and panties down my legs. Why hadn't I known how horny I was? After I'd kicked the last of my clothing aside, he held me for a moment, pressing my skin against the wholesome texture of his cotton shirt and pants—his version of casual wear. When he pressed his lips to mine and slid his tongue between them, he seemed to be making a silent promise: Don't worry, I'll feed you.

I helped him take his clothes off, and I was too impatient to be careful. He seemed to be laughing silently. Sliding his pants down over the bulge at his crotch, I was flattered to feel its hardness. As soon as his cock was released from his jockey shorts (so white they hurt my eyes), it pointed toward me, begging for attention.

To my surprise, Serge slid away from me, and then flung himself on his back onto his luxurious bed, spreading his arms wide. It was a melodramatic gesture that served a practical purpose: with one hand, he reached for a packet on a bedside table, brought it to his mouth, and released a lime-green condom. "Come on," he invited me, grinning with his eyes. I dove on top of him, kissing him teasingly and then sliding my breasts over his surprisingly muscular chest.

"Wait," he told me, reaching beneath to roll the latex sheath over his straining shaft." Won't you sit on it?" he asked, as sweet as a girl but with a certain ironic undercurrent. "Baby?"

"Gladly," I chuckled, "but not yet." I slid down his body until I could take his cock into my mouth, and I discovered a vein that bulged even through the sheath. I teased it with my tongue and probed the underside of the head. I hadn't done this in so long that I felt slightly amazed, as well as reassured, that even the cocks of unusual men behave predictably. Serge stroked my hair in appreciation.

My pussy felt beyond my control, as if it was likely to start drooling onto his clean comforter at any moment. My clit felt almost unbearably touchy, and I could feel a certain maddening itch that longed to be scratched deep inside my lower mouth near my cervix. Somehow my hunger felt dominant and submissive at the same time: I felt as if I could tear walls down, or tie Serge to his own bed, if that's what it took to get what I needed. I also felt as if I would offer him anything in exchange for relief. The dimensions of "anything" could be explored later.

Serge's cock looked thicker than the last one I'd seen, and it bent slightly at an angle. I found it endearing. As I knelt over the impatient animal, its owner smiled serenely at me as if he could wait forever. I grasped the shaft to guide it into me as I slowly slid down on it, feeling it twitch as I watched Serge's expression. He casually reached down with both arms. As I began to move, one of his fingers, slippery with lube, slid into my anus. As I descended on the thick, delicious organ that filled my pussy, the modest finger gained territory alongside it. Serge's other hand held one of my hips as I rode him.

Our dance felt perverse in the best sense. I didn't feel like half of a conventional couple; I felt like a moon goddess playing with her brother, the sun, to make stars. I squeezed him to give pleasure, and was surprised at how much I got in return. The friction of his shaft in my lower mouth seemed to be striking sparks in my clit, and I knew I was going to come before he did. "Ohhh," I sighed, wanting to warn him but unable to put words together.

Serge responded with another unexpected move: He pulled his finger out of my ass so that he could bring both his warm hands to my bouncing breasts. As he rubbed, kneaded, and squeezed them, a pang from each nipple rushed into my guts, filling them with the sweetest sadness. My eyes stung with tears. With a mighty effort, I blinked them back.

"Come on," he encouraged, almost under his breath, "you can let go, honey." I wasn't sure exactly which kind of release he was urging on me, but I was determined not to cry.

For a long, unbearable moment, all my feelings seemed to be centered in my bursting clit. Like a daredevil in a barrel, poised at the top of Niagara Falls, I wondered if I would go over the edge. Then it was happening—my cunt squeezed and squeezed as if it wanted to milk all the juice out of the strange manfruit inside it. I felt as if I could never get enough air into my lungs. Sweat popped up on my skin as more water welled up in my eyes; no part of me was dry.

Serge stayed hard and stayed calm. After my frenzy had somewhat subsided, he resumed pumping to a steady, persistent beat. Wanting to please him, I bent down to kiss his warm mouth, and gently scratched the fine dark hair on his firm chest. Holding both my hips, he settled me on his cock with increasing roughness as his need grew. I squeezed him deliberately with all the art I could summon. Before long, he rose up off the bed to plunge into me as deeply as he could, groaning as a stored load of fluid shot into the snug green bag. I almost wished I could feel his sperm bombarding my womb, its intended goal. "Baby," he sighed, stroking my sweaty back.

"Honey," I sighed back. I couldn't help remembering the last person I had addressed this way. I told myself that the differences between my present and my previous lover were irrelevant; a sweet body, animated by a need to connect, was a gift from the Goddess, who surely created balls and chest hair as well as breasts and clits.

Serge's spent organ began sliding out of me. Reluctantly, I rose up to give it breathing space, and then gently rolled the condom off as he watched me with interest.

"The wastebasket is near the bureau," he advised. I sat up, slid my legs off the end of Serge's luxurious bed, and walked two steps to the wicker object that waited to receive the product of his hunger for me. I was tempted to save it as a souvenir. I wondered whether Serge would be disgusted by my lack of disgust; I was not willing to find out yet.

My lips felt dry as if I'd been crawling through a desert for days. I licked them as Serge watched me. "Lip balm is on the bureau, Sherry," he said in a voice that suggested a desire to smear various exotic substances on me. I went looking for the magic ointment that could make my lips as kissable as I wanted them to be. The confusion of small bottles, jars, tubes, business cards, and envelopes on the bureau posed a delicate moral issue: Did I have the right to rummage through his belongings for the thing he had offered me? An hour ago, the answer to this question would have been clear. Now I wondered if he assumed I was on intimate terms with the minutiae of his life. Glancing quickly over the picturesque mess, I noticed a square envelope decorated with butterflies. It obviously contained a matching greeting card, probably given to him by some smitten man or woman. Then I recognized the return address. It hit me in the stomach like a blow from a lead pipe. Numbly, I kept looking until I found a small jar of lip balm and returned to the bed.

"What's wrong, baby?" Serge asked. He took the jar of lip balm from my fingers, opened it, and carefully smeared some on my mouth. I took a deep breath as he wrapped an arm around my waist. With the same hand that had touched my lips like a butterfly's wing, he slapped my ass. "What is it?" he insisted.

"How do you know Blaine Wishfort?" I blurted. "Why did she send you a card?"

The man looked me in the eyes. "I knew her as 'Janice,'" he told me. "She said 'Blaine' was her middle name. I saw her a few times, Sherry. She told me about you."

I couldn't stand it. "Oh, I bet she did," I answered furiously.

"Sherry," he interrupted. "She didn't blame you for anything. She told me she left you. I think she felt quite guilty about it. I didn't have what she wanted either, and it didn't take her long to figure that out."

"I don't see why she wasn't happy with you," I told him bitterly. "She wanted a man."

"You think so?" he challenged. "No, baby. She was looking for status, power, an image she could attach herself to. She thought I had all that, or I was likely to get it. She didn't want *me*. After I got to know her a little, I realized she wasn't who I thought she was at first." Serge held me, trying to ease the pain I couldn't hide. "The worst thing either of us could wish on her is that she'll get what she's looking for. She probably will. I wish her luck."

I wiped my eyes with one hand. To my chagrin, Serge dabbed at them with a corner of the sheet. "So it didn't take you long?" I demanded sarcastically. "You or her? So I'm the only fool who thought it could work?"

"Why torture yourself, woman?" he asked, rocking me gently. "You thought you saw what you wanted. We all do that. A long time or a short time—what difference does it make?"

I wasn't willing to let it go. "She used to clean my apartment while I was writing. And she'd make me coffee and bake cookies. She said she loved everything I wrote. She would take my manuscripts to the post office to send off. I should have known: It was too good to trust."

Serge brushed my hair away from my face, exposing what I didn't want him to see. I jerked back. "Mmm," he murmured consolingly. "Sherry. She told me how much she admired you."

This comment almost made me puke. "She believed in me, she said. Believed in what? If she really thought I was ever going to become rich and famous, she was a worse fool than I was for believing that we…" I couldn't say it.

Serge knew. "She told me she wanted to move in with you, keep house for you."

Now my humiliation was complete. "As if any sane person really wants to be a wife nowadays. Did she offer to do that for you?"

Serge chuckled. "Baby, we would have killed each other. She wanted to redecorate this place. I had to set her straight." I couldn't help laughing, although it hurt my heart.

The pain of loss still flowed nauseatingly through my guts as Serge slid me beneath him and lay on top of me, resting on his elbows. He slid down and licked my nipples like a cat. "Such beautiful breasts, honey," he said. "Do you ever show cleavage?"

I guffawed. "Where, Serge, at the library? At..." I censored my thought in time. "No."

"I know you go to the gay bar," he remarked casually, tweaking my nipples to make them rock hard. "I've seen real women with cleavage in there. It's not a crime. You've got it, you might as well flaunt it." I was growing too hungry again to argue.

One of Serge's hands snaked down to my pubic hair. Two comic fingers strutted through it, marching down to find my clit and distract me from the past while tickling my resistance away. Before that could happen, I wanted him to know what I was thinking.

"Listen," I told him, grabbing the mischievous hand. "I won't wear a dead man's evening gown. I won't. But I might wear something else. I'm sorry I was so abrupt when you told me about Dick. I'm sorry you lost him. It must have been terrible. Was he sick for a long time?" I've never been known for my tact or my timing.

Serge sighed and lay his head on my upper chest for a moment before answering. "It was a car accident, honey," he informed me quietly. "Totally unexpected. I was driving."

"Jesus," I reacted without thinking. "I'm sure it wasn't your fault."

"It wasn't," he sighed, "according to the insurance company. I know that in my head." I kissed his forehead, his nose, his cheeks, wanting to kiss away the mess of tangled emotions, knowing I couldn't do it.

"It's OK," he lied. His mouth searched for mine and found it. The warm, soft pressure of his lips on mine sent a message directly to my now-neglected clit. I wiggled slightly beneath his half-awakened cock. He paused for breath. "I got a lot of emotional support at the time," he assured me. "Thank the

Goddess for my women friends." This reference to the deity of my faith sounded very strange coming from him, but then I thought, *Why not?*

I laughed, reaching down to find his sensitive joystick, like a live toy that was permanently attached to his flesh and his feelings. I didn't envy him for having it, but I loved what it could do for me. "Well, thank the horned god of all horny animals for this," I told him. "And the rest of you," I added generously.

Serge was determined to find my clit before I could encourage his willful cock to plunge into me again. "So crude," he clucked. "So natural and unpolished. What can I do with you?"

His question didn't seem to need an answer. He stroked and teased my clit into a swollen state of excitement. "Is this unfair?" he demanded suddenly, knowing I couldn't think clearly.

"Yes," I laughed breathlessly. I knew his fingers were now coated with my fluid. "But maybe I'm using you too," I shot back while I still could.

"I can live with that, honey," he said, rising up gracefully to reach for another lime-green coat for his demanding cock.

I felt as if I could melt when he guided it into my hungry, shameless cunt. As I pulled him into me with all my will, the smell of his cologne came to my nose in gusts, mixed with the rich smell of our bodies. I hoped I could satisfy him as well as I knew he would satisfy me.

I felt as if my life had entered a cycle that was spinning me out of control. I didn't know where I would be when it ended, but for now I was loving the ride.

SOMETHING FOR THE PAIN

Amelia G

SOMEHOW IT SEEMS WRONG TO ME THAT HAVING sold my screenplay means I can afford to go to the dentist. Writing the screenplay was fun even if the cross-country drive and the irritating Hollywood parties weren't. Going to the dentist, now *that* is something I should get paid a lot for enduring. Scripting a science-fiction spectacular, which was to star one of my favorite actresses—now that is *not* something that should put six figures in my bank account.

I contemplated this injustice as I waited in the oral surgeon's office. I'd gone for so long without dental care while I was working on the screenplay, making it perfect. I was aware at the time that the pain in my mouth had become a constant in my life, but it wasn't really a big thing. You can get used to anything. Julie offered to front me the money to go and get it taken care of, but I didn't want to sponge off her. So I let it go and let it go, and by the time I finally went to the dentist, he informed me that I had an infection in the bones of my jaw. Actually, from the left side of my chin up through my right ear.

Apparently dentists can discover such things, but even they find them too disgusting to deal with. So my dentist recommended an oral surgeon. Only, of course, this is L.A.—and the oral surgeon just couldn't fit me in. So I called my agent at CAA and she set the oral surgeon straight and he said he could squeeze me in after all.

Apparently Dr. Levinthal—*that's* "Dr. Noah" *in Hollywood speak*—is the best at what he does. A sought-after guy. Not just anyone can get him to pull out their teeth and hollow out their jaw bones. You have to be a Somebody to get a marrow transplant from Dr. Noah. His waiting room featured autographed photographs of some of his celebrity clients. Jay Leno. Nick Nolte. Sylvester Stallone. Janet Jackson. And, oh, be still my beating heart, he had a personalized autographed Gina Gershon publicity still, complete with ridiculously flattering thanks. *Bound* was Julie's and my favorite movie.

The nurse came out and told me I could come in, and I considered telling her I wasn't Bobbie Logan. Nope, Bobbie Logan is a Somebody and I'm just me. Besides, Bobbie Logan has an appointment with the oral surgeon and I'm certain I don't. OK, OK, my name *is* Bobbie Logan. I just don't like hearing dental assistants say it. I took a deep breath and went inside.

"Call me Dr. Noah," the surgeon told me as he clasped my hand warmly.

"I'm Bobbie. Hi." I gave him a weak smile and sat down in the chair, folding my hands over my lap so that he wouldn't see them shake. I wondered if maybe I should have asked for a recommendation for a female surgeon.

I guess to distract and relax me, Dr. Noah and his assistant tried to converse with me while he poked around in my mouth.

"So I understand you're from Atlanta," the doctor said.

"I hear it's beautiful there," the assistant chimed in. "Do you miss it?"

"Uhgrl."

"A little," said Dr. Noah as he stuck a piece of black rubber roughly the size of the state of California into my mouth. "You only miss it a little?" The way he said it made the question seem sympathetically probing and sweet.

"Uhl I eh uh-uhn ee-in. I urln."

"What?" asked the assistant.

Dr. Noah had about six different weird metal tools in my mouth, but he looked up from his work and told his helper, "She said she left someone behind."

"Oh, are you married? Husband? Boyfriend?"

I guess I looked a little wild-eyed at that because Dr. Noah patted my hand comfortingly as he said, "No, no, she said her girlfriend." I'm used to prejudice from living in Georgia, but I've found that bigots in California are at least a little shy about their pig-ignorant views. They have to get to know you before they spout off about which minorities they hate. Usually, Californians lower their voices slightly when spouting. Not that Dr. Noah seemed to have any issues with my having had a girlfriend in some other state. The really odd thing was that he could understand exactly what I was saying with all that junk in my mouth. Positively supernatural.

"That's nice," the assistant said. It wasn't nice at all, actually, but it didn't sound like Dr. Noah's assistant meant anything sarcastic.

"It looks like you've had some good prep work done here," Dr. Noah told me, as he used one of his little metal implements to prod one of my molars.

I love hard-boiled novels, and I'd always read books where the hero gets conked on the head and pain blossoms or explodes in his skull—but I never really knew what it felt like before this.

"Oh, I ah! Ah ur!"

"That's OK, Bobbie. I'm sorry that hurt." The doctor's voice was soothing, but this hurt too much to be soothed verbally. He gave me three shots in quick succession, but minutes later I was still panting from the pain.

"Ih ee uh-ung or!" I reached up and tore the black plastic out of my mouth. Trying not to shriek, I told him, "Give me something more!"

"I heard you the first time, Bobbie. Relax." He fitted a little mask over my nose and told me to breathe in through my nose and out through my mouth. It still hurt like a bitch, but I started to mind less. The doctor gave me eight more injections, but they didn't seem that bothersome. The pain became bearable. I breathed deeply.

I saw her boots first. They were fabulous, stiletto-heeled confections of thick latex, with rows of metal spikes on the outside of her calves and zippers on the inside for that extra-tight fit. She was standing with her back to me, and I saw the black latex dildos sprouting from her heels. I stuck out my tongue and put the tip to one of the shining black dildos. A flavor like cherry-mint cola burst through my tongue, suffusing my senses.

She turned around, and I moved my gaze from her shoes to the rest of her. She was almost completely encased in shiny black latex, but not in a submissive way. There were big metal spikes around her neck and wrists and a variety of zippers and straps across her body.

She wore a gleaming black strap-on jutting from her crotch.

Julie liked to use a strap-on on me, but she never let me return the favor. It was just like her to want to take care of me, but not want me to take care of her. It's the main reason I'm reluctant to fly her out here. On the one hand, I don't suppose she is that attached to her job at the jack shack, spending the day saying, "Oooooh yeah baby, that'll be another $100, take a look at this, no I can't touch it for you, but feel free to make yourself more comfortable." She'd probably change her mind and be willing to fly out here if she didn't have to pay for it. On the other hand, I can't help but feel resentful that Julie tried to convince me not to come out to L.A., not to follow my dream, not to get to where I could take care of myself.

The woman in black carried a bull whip, and her head was cloaked in an entirely implausible helmet with face mask. Two black dildos like her strap-on, but decorated with metal spikes, sprang from the sides of her head like antlers. They might have looked foolish on someone else, but, so help me, they looked hot on her, perhaps because they framed her eyes. Peering out over a Darth Vader–style gas mask, her eyes were huge, luminous, hypnotic. Somehow, the fact that the windows to her soul were the only part of her that was exposed made them that much sexier.

"Take off your clothes." Her voice sounded kind of like Darth Vader meets Lauren Bacall.

"What? No. Where am I?"

She shrugged. "If there is somewhere you'd rather be...."

Abruptly I felt the most intense pain I have ever experienced lance through the right side of my face.

"Dr. Noah, I think she's coming out of it."

The pain was so strong, it was not just pain but unbearable waves of heat throbbing in my head. I think I may have screamed. A horror movie scream. Like please let this not be happening to me.

Then slowly the cool salve of cherry mint spread from my tongue through my head and I was back in the white room with the woman in black latex. This time I was quick to pull off my tank top, unlace my combat boots, and drag my new black jeans down to the ground.

I've got a tight, compact body and I don't have to bother with underwear, so I don't. (Actually, I was just too broke to spend money on stuff like bras or whatever for a long time, and then when I was suddenly flush, I realized I didn't like underwear anymore.)

"Bend over and present that nice little ass to me," she instructed.

Mutely I obeyed.

I shuddered with pleasure at the first touch of her latex-clad index finger on my cunt. "Aren't you a juicy morsel?" she purred. "I'd definitely like to take your pain away. But, first, a little test." Then, abruptly, she shoved the handle of her bull whip into my cunt, hard. I was wet but not dripping, not totally ready for it, and it was fairly big, and though it was rubber, the handle was woven and rough, and it hurt a little bit, so I cried out.

"Just tell me if you don't like it," the woman in shining black said. When I did not reply, she went on. "OK, get down on all fours and give me four laps around this room with that tail trailing behind you. Come on now, crawl for me. We've got some time to kill."

So I began to crawl around the white cell. The walls were white and the floor was white and the ceiling was white, and there seemed to be something wrong with the geometry of the room somehow. The room sort of gave me vertigo, but I was distracted, as each time I moved my hands and knees, it stimulated me where the whip handle protruded. It was like that whip handle was sized just for me, a little too big to be comfortable, a pleasure I had to stretch and grow into. Each time I snuck a glance up at my dildo-antlered ruler, I felt joy and the sensation of a cherry-mint taste in parts of my body that should not be able to detect flavor at all.

I think I might have succeeded in doing the four laps around that room if I hadn't gotten so wet so fast or if the room hadn't seemed to change in shape and size as I traversed it. At any rate, I only managed to do about two-and-a-half circuits.

"Tsk, tsk," she scolded, "now we will have to use up the time with other pursuits." I tensed when she picked up the bull whip. It was a big whip, the length of it proportionate with the size of its handle. "No, darling, I'm not going to strike you with this. I can tell that is not what you want, what you like, what you need." I turned to look at her, and she prodded me with the toe of one of her sleek, heavy latex boots.

"Come on now, I want you leaning over my little horsey, pronto." Her huge gray eyes were so beautiful, I wanted to ask her to take off the gas mask so that I could see the rest of her face. But I was afraid that perhaps her eyes were her only truly striking feature. Or perhaps she had no true human flesh other than that around her eyes. Anyway, I loved that Darth Vader–meets–Lauren Bacall voice. I wish more women spoke like that.

She leaned over and swatted my ass with one gloved hand. "Come on, over the horse now." A gymnast's horse had appeared in the white room. I had not noticed it when I was crawling around, but perhaps my mind had been focused on the persistent, sexy throb between my legs. I got up and bent over the horse and immediately felt one of her hands smack my ass and then rest there, massaging gently. The impact sent a shock of excitement through me. She poked at my lips with one finger, spreading me wide open for whatever she had in mind. "You are very, very wet, my dear," her incredible voice rasped.

"Yes," I choked out, "but how can you tell with those gloves on?"

"I am aware of your needs, your feelings, and my sensations are...irrelevant. Besides, you are dripping and I have eyes."

"Oh."

"What would you like?" she inquired, as pleasantly as some-one who sounds like Darth Vader can. She pressed the tip of her strap-on dildo to my cunt, but would not insert it despite my frantic wriggling. I felt a minty sensation at my entrance.

"Put it in," I hissed, pressing back against her. "Put it in now."

"Are you sure?" She giggled through the mask and swatted my ass with her free hand again. "Will that be distracting enough?"

"Please."

Roughly she spread me open wider with both gloved hands and shoved her black dildo all the way into me in one smooth motion. I gasped as she held still, waiting for my body to become accustomed to the large intruder. The business with the whip handle had readied me, though, and it felt very fine indeed. I began to squirm, and she pumped easily in and out of me. I felt as if I could taste artificial cherries and mints in my cunt, but more than that, I wanted to come. I was a taut piece of machinery about to blow up.

"My clit," I gasped, "rub my clit too."

"Like this?" she purred raspily, as she continued to thrust and reached around to press where I'd requested. Almost immediately after her hand touched my clit, I exploded into a million intensely pleased pieces.

When I came out from under, I felt not quite nauseated but a little queasy, as if I might start feeling nauseated at any moment. "You're going to be just fine," Dr. Noah told me in his sweet, soothing doctor voice. "I'm going to give you something more for the pain. My receptionist will give you the prescription on your way out."

I nodded my understanding and was immediately sorry. I might still be numbed up, but moving my head too briskly was definitely not pleasant.

The receptionist was cute, with a blonde buzz cut, and she tripped my gay-dar at least a little. Could have just been wishful thinking, though. I thought about asking her what was fun to do around here. I know where to go in Los Angeles to sell my writing for monumental sums, but I have no clue what to do for a good time. I contemplated whether the receptionist might be straight while I wrote out the check for services performed today. I still felt wonder at my good fortune every time I wrote out a check for any large amount. As I handed the receptionist the check, I made eye contact. Nope, straight, I think.

Didn't matter. It felt as if half of my face must be horribly swollen from the oral surgery, so even if she was a dyke, she probably wouldn't be attracted to me. Now that the phone in my new apartment was turned on, maybe I would just try to call Julie again when I got home. I wished I knew what I wanted to do. I've lived so much of my life doing what I had to do, because there was little or no choice. But now those six digits on my ATM receipts mean that I have a choice, only I don't know what I want. Never gave it that much thought before. There is a reason my screenplay is big-budget action-adventure, not art-house introspection.

I think maybe I'll just take my nice new prescription to the pharmacy downstairs, get it filled and go to my new home, masturbate to M2, and enjoy the fact that I don't have to endure the pain any more. Unless I want to.

EGGS McMENOPAUSE

Lesléa Newman

INSOMNIA EQUALS INSANITY. AND BELIEVE ME, I should know. I haven't slept in two years. *Two years.* Ever since September 10th, 1996, when my period stopped on a dime. Damn. Who knew I was out of eggs? Not me. It's not as if I got any kind of warning or anything. One month there I was, bleeding away like a stuck pig, and the next month—bam!—dry as a bone.

So the question is, would I have done anything differently had I known? Thrown myself a party? Saved my last bit of menstrual blood in a jar like Paul Newman's spaghetti sauce? Found some guy to fuck at the Last Chance Motel so that I could finally be a mother once and for all? Not that I ever wanted to be a mother, you understand. It's just that once I knew I couldn't be, all of a sudden, that's exactly what I wanted to do: Grow big as a house. Give birth. Breast-feed. The whole nine yards. It was ridiculous. Sort of like pining away for a lover after you've broken up with her. You know how it is—you don't want to be with her anymore, *you're* the one who called it quits, you can't even stand the fucking sight of her—but as soon as she has her arm around somebody else's waist, you want her as much as you've ever wanted anybody in your whole life. *More.* And if you make the mistake of telling her that, and if she makes the mistake of running back to you, then—poof!—your desire disappears as finally and completely as my last egg. That's human nature for ya. We want what we don't have until we get it, and then we don't want it anymore.

Like my period. God, when I was a teenager, I was dying to get my period. I was the last kid in my class to get it. All the other girls wore their sanitary napkins like badges. "I can't have gym today, Miss Allbright. I have *my friend*," they'd say in a stage whisper loud enough for all the other girls to hear. They carried their bodies differently, too. As if they had some holy wisdom between their legs that I was just dying to get my hands on. *Please,* I'd pray every night before bed. *Please, I'll do anything, just let me get my period. Please.* I'd rush to the bathroom every morning, shut my eyes, and listen to the sweet music of my pee hitting the toilet water. Then I'd take a deep breath, wipe, and open my eyes. But every day that pink toilet paper came up with *nada.*

Then one morning I pulled down my pajamas, and before I even sat down on the pot, I saw they were stained with thick, brown blood. I was so surprised, I didn't even know what it was. I thought I was dying. I had no idea how I cut myself down there, as I didn't spend any time down there at all, much less with a sharp instrument. I told my mother, and she slapped me. Twice. Slap-slap, once on each cheek. It's a Jewish custom, though it's also a custom not to tell you it's a custom, so of course I thought I had just done one more thing to make my mother mad. After the slaps, she gave me a belt and a sanitary napkin and told me to be careful, I was a woman now, and I'd bleed once a month until I was at least 50, so I'd better watch myself, soon all the boys would be after me.

Well, she was partly right, my mother. I did bleed until I was 50, but the boys were never after me. The girls were after me, or, to be more precise, I was after the girls. Girls with their periods, girls without their periods, tall girls, short girls, fat girls, thin girls, I didn't care. I wasn't fussy. I just wasn't happy unless I had some sweet, warm, female thing in my arms. Which I haven't had, in case you're wondering, for a long, long time.

It's not that I'm a dog or anything, you understand. It's just that menopause, in case you haven't gone through it yet, doesn't make you feel like you're the most attractive woman in the world. First of all, you bloat. I looked in the mirror one day and thought, damn, who the hell snuck in here when I wasn't looking and injected helium under my skin? I looked like a balloon from the goddamn Macy's Thanksgiving Day Parade. Second of all, you sweat. Night sweats, day sweats, morning, afternoon, evening sweats. God, I grew hotter than hell and didn't wear a winter coat for two whole years, and New York City in fucking February isn't exactly Miami in July. I couldn't bear the thought of anyone coming near me; in fact, I could hardly stand to be near myself. And on top of all this, I got pimples—pimples!—at my age. I looked like a walking, talking member of Acne Anonymous. And then of course I was so sleep-deprived, I could have walked right past Miss America (who happens to be just my type), and I wouldn't even have noticed.

So one night when I couldn't sleep, I started doing the math. I got my period when I was 16, and it stopped when I was 50. That's 34 years, times 12 months a year, equals 408 periods. And 408 eggs. You could make the world's biggest omelet. Or something.

Call me crazy, but I got obsessed with the number. Four-hundred-and-eight. They say your ovaries are the size of two tiny almonds, so how could they hold 204 eggs apiece? That's a lotta eggs. Being a visual gal, I wanted to see them. I wanted to feel them. So I bought them. Went down to the corner store and bought 34 dozen eggs. A few dozen at a time. I might be crazy all right, but I don't want the whole neighborhood knowing just how loony I am. Luckily, I live in New York, where there's a corner store on every corner. I just worked the neighborhood and bought a few dozen here, a few dozen there.

At first I just stacked the cartons one on top of the other in the living room. Four stacks in the corner; two stacks of eight dozen, two stacks of nine. To tell you the truth, I was a little afraid of them. I had to live with them for a while—you know, get used to them. I mean, to my mind, they represented my unborn children, in a twisted sort of way. I even started naming them. Went right through the alphabet: Annie, Bonnie, Carol, Delilah, Ellen, Francis, Grace. You get the picture. Then I started in with boys' names: Adam, Barry, Carlos, David, Eddie, Frankie, Greg. I had to do it 15 fucking times. Abigail, Betty, Claire, Deborah… Allen, Burt, Craig, Daniel… Amy, Barbara… Angel, Bernie… Pretty sick, huh? That's nothing compared to what I did next.

Next, I unpacked them and started placing them around the apartment. Now if you've never been up here, let me tell you, this place ain't exactly The Plaza. It's pretty tiny, just three small rooms, and I haven't redecorated in a while. Since the Ice Age, as a matter of fact. But I'm not complaining. My hovel is perfect for one person. One crazy person and her 408 eggs.

The first place I put them was on the couch. Eight dozen fit there, and another eight fit on the bed. Three dozen covered my kitchen table, and two dozen filled the shower. A dozen fit in the bathroom sink, and another dozen filled the sink in the kitchen. Twenty-three down and 11 to go. I had no choice, then, but to lay them out on the floor. It looked kind of like an inside-out Yellow Brick Road. The floor was covered with eggs except for a twisted, windy path that led from the bedroom through the living room, through the kitchen, and out the front door.

When I was finally finished—I have to say it—I felt pretty damn proud. Sure I had used up my eggs—nothing much to it, women do that all the time—but how many women have actually *replaced* them? I stood in the narrow path in my apartment, looked around, and felt smug. For about two seconds. And then I started feeling incredibly horny. All those eggs! I mean, have you ever felt an egg, I mean really *felt* an egg? They're very sensual, you know. They've got a little weight to them; they're heavy and smooth, not unlike a woman's breast that fits just right in the palm of your hand. I took two eggs off the floor and held one in each paw for a minute, closing my eyes and just bouncing them up and down a little. God, I felt like a cat in heat. No, not a cat, a pussy. I wanted some, and I wanted it *now*.

So what could I do? *Go out, you old fool,* I said to myself. I hadn't been out for about a million years, and the thought of it was more than a little daunting. Had I lost my charm? (Had I ever had it?) There was only one way to find out. Go out. So I did. I got all dressed up in a jacket and tie, did something with my hair, put on my motorcycle boots, and hit the street. I didn't even know if the bar I used to haunt was still there—part of me prayed it wasn't, and part of me prayed it was. I heard the disco beat half a block away, and it pulled me inside like a magnet. God, it felt good to be out with the girls.

Now before you jump all over me and tell me I should be calling them women, let me tell you, these were *girls*. To my mind, anyway. I wasn't quite old enough to be their mother, you understand. I was old enough to be their grandmother. Sure, you do the math. Eighteen and 18 is 36, plus 18 more is 54.

Which is just a year and a half shy of how old I was. And how shy. I almost turned around and marched out the door the second after I marched in, but traffic was going against me, so I went with the flow and headed straight (so to speak) inside. I mean, what the hell, I had dragged myself out of the house, and there was no one back there waiting for me but the ingredients for about 200 Egg McMuffins. I might as well pretend to enjoy myself.

I headed for the bar and parked on an empty stool. Asked the bartender for whatever was on tap, leaned back on my elbows, and looked around. Luckily I didn't have to look far. There were two gals to my right, one more gorgeous than the other. Were they together? It was hard to tell. Both of them were dressed in black from head to toe: black sweaters, black stockings, black skirts, black shoes. So I doubted they were lovers, because, after all, what can two femmes do together? But then again, this is a new generation. Femmes go with femmes, butches go with butches—hell, I've even heard that the newest "happenin'" thing is for girls to go with boys. Although what's so new and radical about that is beyond my imagination.

I pretended I didn't notice the two babes, of course, but I kept my eye on them and tried to eavesdrop on their conversation. Easier said than done, as the music was really pumping, and though I hate to admit it, my hearing isn't what it used to be. I can't believe I'm turning into one of those old sows who walk into a bar and whine, "Why does the music have to be so loud? Can't they turn it do-ow-ow-own?" But as I've already told you, age does strange things to a person. So I couldn't really hear, but I could see all right, and let me tell you, both these broads were drop-dead gorgeous. One of them had that short, bleached-out blonde, rhinestone glasses, dog-collar-around-the-neck look. Very East Village, not exactly my type. The other one, though, I'd lick her boots any day. She had long black hair down to her waist, and she was at least six feet tall, even without the five-inch platform shoes. God, her legs went on forever, and I couldn't stand that they weren't wrapped around my waist that very minute. But before I could even ask the bartender what she was drinking so I could send one over with my compliments (a move that makes them swoon, or at least did in the old days), she turned from her gal-pal, tossed all that glorious hair over her shoulder in a huff, and flounced into the crowd.

Now let me tell you, if there's one thing I love even more than dykes, it's dyke drama. I sidled up to Miss St. Mark's Place and asked, "Is she your girlfriend?"

"Why don't you ask her?" She pointed to the object of my affection, who had obviously changed her mind.

Well, I always was one to follow orders. Pointing to the blonde, I asked the goddess standing before me, "Is she your girlfriend?"

"What did she say when you asked *her?*" Mademoiselle thrust her fists onto her hips and looked at me with blazing eyes.

This was beginning to feel like therapy; every question I asked was being answered with another question. "She said to ask you." I looked the towering Glamazon in the eye and held her gaze as she snorted and shook her head. "C'mon." She held out her hand, to my delight and amazement. "Let's dance."

Well, she sure didn't have to ask me twice. I slid off that bar stool like a greased pig and let her lead me to the dance floor where I attempted to move these old bones to the music, if you could call it that. All I could hear was some kind of throbbing, pumping techno beat. Perfect for humping, I thought, and as if my girl had a Ph.D. in mind-reading, she pulled me into her and started working away. I hate to admit it, but my knees actually buckled, and I had to hold on for dear life. Luckily there was a lot to hold onto. Like I told you, this girl was beyond tall. Her crotch came up to my hip bone, and her breasts were at eye level. I smelled her sweat and her juice and her perfume, and just kept my hip jutted out so that she could go to town. "Ooh, baby, you are something else," I murmured and somehow found her nipple in my mouth. Cashmere never tasted so good, let me tell you. A few times I tried to look up at my dancing damsel, but either her eyes were closed or they were focused in the direction of the bar. Was she using me to make her girlfriend jealous? Did I care? Hey, a revenge fuck was better than a mercy fuck, though to tell you the truth, from this babe-and-a-half, I'd have taken either.

When the music changed, we headed back toward the bar, but much to my relief, the Blonde Bombshell was gone. I couldn't tell if Mandy was pissed, relieved, or disappointed. (Once her come was all over my jeans, I figured I had the right to ask her name.) Without a word, she hopped up on that still-warm barstool, drained what was left of her gal-pal's drink, and drew me toward her by wrapping those mile-long legs around the base of my butt. I felt her muscles clench as she held me tightly, and I realized I couldn't get away even if I wanted to. Which I didn't, in case you're wondering. I may have gone bananas in other departments, but I wasn't so far gone that I'd look this gift horse in the mouth.

"You live around here, baby?" Mandy whispered, letting her tongue roam the highways and byways of my grateful left ear.

"Just a few blocks away," I panted, and let me tell you, it was a good thing she had me by the butt because my legs were beyond Jell-O.

"Let's go." She released me, and I commanded my skeletal system to get a grip as we made our way out the door. Once outside, I tried to lean her against a lamppost and kiss her a bit, but it was embarrassing for her to have to bend down an entire foot just to get her mouth anywhere near mine. Clearly I had to get this girl on her back as quickly as possible, so we hustled down the street and up the steps to my apartment. I thought of carrying her over the threshold, but when I opened the door, I couldn't believe my eyes. The eggs! I had forgotten all about them. Would she notice? I decided to play it cool, since after all, what other choice did I have?

"Walk this way," I said, bending over like Groucho Marx and waddling down the narrow path to my bed, which was of course completely covered with eggs. I thought of whipping away the bedspread, like a magician who can pull a tablecloth out from under plates, glasses, and silverware without disturbing them, but that would have been too dramatic. Besides, it wouldn't have worked.

But Mandy, bless her heart, was foolish with youth, liquid courage, or just a wacky sense of humor. "The yolk's on you," she said, reaching for an egg that she cracked with one hand on the bed frame like a young, beautiful Julia Child. Then she deposited the contents of the shell expertly and neatly right on top of my head.

"Allow me," I said, and with cool yolk dripping down the side of my face and neck, I sent all eight dozen of those babies flying with one grand, gallant sweep of my arm. As they rolled, cracked, and crashed to the ground, I prayed Mandy wouldn't forsake me and run screaming out the door. But not too worry. I sure know how to pick 'em, if I do say so myself. Mandy just flopped down on the now-clear bed and rolled onto her back, with her hands behind her head and a look that said loud and clear, *OK, I've done my job; now it's up to you.* God, I love those femmes.

"Over easy," I remarked as I bent down to unbutton her sweater. She wore no bra, and damned if her breasts didn't remind me of two eggs sunny side up. I cracked an egg onto her chest and licked her nipples through the yellow goo. She laughed and opened her legs, which had somehow worked their way out of her skirt. Crotchless pantyhose—what will they think of next? Clearly Mandy had been expecting to get some action that night, but being fucked with an organic egg by a butch three times her age probably wasn't exactly what she had in mind.

I moved the lucky egg slowly up one magnificent thigh until it was right up against the path to glory. I pressed it against her and rolled it around and around until the shell was slippery and slick. "You move, it breaks," I said, teasing her clit with the tip of it.

"It breaks, you eat it," she replied, squeezing her legs together and cracking that ova in two.

Well, suffice it to say, my cholesterol level skyrocketed that night clear through the fucking roof. I had egg on my face, and I didn't mind it one bit. We crunched our way through my entire apartment, and that Mandy wasn't squeamish in the least. I licked egg off her toes, off her nose.... We fucked in every room, and by morning there wasn't an egg left to scramble. Four-hundred-and-eight eggs smashed to smithereens. That's gotta be worthy of the *Guinness Book of World Records,* don't you think? I tell you, I was so spent by the time the sun came up, I didn't know if I was wide awake or dreaming. I shut my baby blues and didn't open them again until later that evening when I woke up alone in my bed, fresh and clean as a new-born chick. Mandy and the eggs were gone, and so were the bags under my eyes. I blinked a few times, wondering if I had imagined the whole thing. Was it all just part of some deranged, menopausal fantasy? I stumbled into the kitchen, where my question was answered in the form of a note I found on the kitchen table: "Thanks for an *eggs-citing* evening. Love, M." The note was anchored by one perfectly round, white egg, upon which Mandy had drawn a goofy smiley face with a blue magic marker. And even though eggs were the last thing I wanted, I'd worked up such an appetite from last night's activities, I cracked that sucker in two and fried it up on the spot. And I tell you, it was the most delicious thing I'd ever eaten in my entire damn life.

SANTA'S LITTLE HELPER

Jenesi Ash

This will be the last time, CERISE PROMISED HERSELF. *One more, and I'll stop for good.*

Cerise sat in her car, listening to the Mormon Tabernacle Choir singing "Silent Night" on the radio. Dusk was approaching, and the outdoor lights glittered in the sunset as her silver Lexus idled in the mall parking lot, facing the decorated storefront. Garlands were draped in lush, dark-green swags over the entrance, secured with giant silver bows, and spangled with tiny white lights that flickered like lightning bugs among the piney boughs. Customers hurried in and out, bumping each other with overflowing shopping bags. But none of this interested Cerise.

Her eyes zeroed in on the man standing by the double glass doors. She watched as he pounded his black-booted feet on the gray pavement, warding off the bitter cold. He rang a brass bell as passers-by dropped coins into his red metal bucket, and he chuckled genially at something a toddler said in passing, his belly shaking under the velvet red suit like the bowlful of jelly it was supposed to be. Cerise's pulse quickened. She had to have him.

This Santa looked like the real thing. His snowy white hair had a natural-looking gloss, curling against the thick collar of his suit. The full, well-trimmed beard looked soft and thick, cascading down the front of his jacket. But most important, this Santa didn't have padding on under his red plush suit. After studying countless Saint Nicks, Cerise considered herself an expert on such matters. This man had the chubby cheeks and stubby, wide hands that promised a gratifyingly genuine Father Christmas. His arms and legs were rounded, his shoulders a little curved. His solid tummy bulged slightly, enticingly, over his large black leather belt.

Cerise sighed. He was *perfect*. But would he be interested? She checked her appearance in the rear-view mirror and wrinkled her nose. Her dark red hair was styled in a soft, conservative pageboy. Her face wasn't pretty or in any way dramatic. Just Midwestern, nondescript. She was neither glamorously voluptuous nor fashionably, super-model thin. She pouted in the mirror, but still she looked like the perfect corporate wife she was. Cerise didn't draw undue attention, always dressing fashionably but appropriately. She wasn't overtly sexy or desirable, which suited her ambitious husband just fine, since it meant no complications with oversexed colleagues or bitchy trophy wives. That kind of thing could break a guy's rise to the top.

Cerise knew she couldn't rely on her looks to get the attention of the jolly old elf: She had to be brazen. Sometimes her bold moves had surprised the unsuspecting Santas, but other times they were pleased. A few times they'd been horrified. A scarlet blush flashed over Cerise's cheeks as she remembered the last one. She cringed. It had hurt—it had—to have her blatant proposition met with such wintry-cold disgust. He'd made her feel like a pervert.

Cerise was ashamed of her secret Santa fetish, of course. It wasn't as if she could make it public. Santa would never grace the walls of sorority dorm rooms except from Thanksgiving to New Year's, and then only on the front of greetings cards tacked to bulletin boards. No one ever said, "I want to jump Santa's bones."

How many times had she been forced to listen to her friends drooling over Tom Cruise and Brad Pitt? Cerise never understood the fascination for these Hollywood celebrities. Tom and Brad were too skinny, too wimpy for her taste. She wanted to sink into a man and sculpt his flesh with her hands. She wanted someone to cover and surround her, shroud her with his body heat. If she never had to hear again, in great detail, what various women of her acquaintance would like to do to famous men, she would be happy. Cerise found the young ones so bland. *Give me someone older. Experienced. None of these Leonardo DiCaprios,* she mused, blanching at the thought of the teen heartthrob's barely postpubescent face. Yuck.

Some of the older "society" women rhapsodized about Sean Connery; Cerise could almost understand that. Sean was looking pretty good in *The Hunt for Red October*. And if he gained some weight...better yet, if Brando grew a beard...ohhh, baby! Heat flashed through Cerise's body as she imagined the older, heavier Brando unshaven. Did any other woman share her feelings? Most people clucked their tongues about how fat he'd gotten, as if they wished he would remain the same age and size he'd been in the '50s. Cerise found the current model infinitely more appealing. Was she the only one who did? Maybe she was. Maybe she was the only woman who was attracted to older, heavier men. What would those women who wet their pants over Brad Pitt say if Cerise described her Santa Claus fantasies? She knew—which was why she never did.

They would think she was a freak.

Maybe she was the only woman on the planet who had a Santa Claus fetish, who considered Santa the sexiest man alive. Did any other women fantasize about Burl Ives in a red velour suit? Cerise was probably the only person on earth who had ever masturbated while watching *Miracle on 34th Street*.

Cerise had tried to control her desires. She didn't want to be different, especially this way. It was so taboo. She'd tried to dissect her obsession, having one-night stands with older men, dating men with white or blond beards. She'd seduced overweight men and flirted with guys wearing red coats. She practically stalked men who combined these characteristics. Yet every one of these men left her wanting. It was just never quite as good, never as fulfilling, if the guy wasn't wearing a Santa suit.

Cerise vividly remembered her first sexual encounter with a Santa Claus. It was three years ago at her husband's company Christmas party, and whoever had planned the party had hired someone who looked and acted like Santa straight out of Clement Clark Moore. She'd ogled him, but that St. Nick hadn't paid any special attention to her—until the party was in full swing.

Then, while nearly everyone else was drunk and Cerise's husband was in his office fucking his former-lingerie-model secretary, Santa cornered her next to the drinking fountains. The hall was empty and shadowy, but Cerise could hear the party in the next room as Santa meshed his body with hers, pressing her against the corporate-mauve wallpaper.

The encounter had been brief, primitive. Cerise loved it. It felt so wicked to fuck one of the world's most beloved children's characters. A part of her wanted to be discovered, to get caught, even by her husband, while she was tangled in Santa's red velveteen trousers.

Ever since then, she'd been desperate to repeat the experience, to recapture the wild excitement. Cerise trolled the shopping malls: Finding the right Santa was almost a part-time job. After disappointing encounters with several college-age Santas, Cerise came to realize that the man had to be the perfect replica of the Christmas icon. Otherwise it wouldn't be the same.

What if there were washboard abs under a pillow inside that coat? What a travesty! But no, this man at the mall certainly *looked* like Santa Claus. Cerise wanted to approach him. But what if he laughed? What if he said no? Worse, what if he sneered and called her a pervert?

Cerise bit her lip, undecided. She didn't think she could suffer another self-righteous Santa. Even if this *was* the last time. Then Santa started singing *Frosty the Snowman*. His jowls, almost concealed by the lustrous beard, quavered slightly. Cerise's body tightened. She had to have him. Immediately.

She turned off the engine and dropped the keys into her black leather handbag, gathered a few coins from the console, and closed the driver's door with a determined click. Shivering from the cold, she pulled her long black fur coat tighter around her body. The frigid wind swirled underneath; she was naked beneath the mink. All she wore were a pair of black suede Maud Frizons, a gleaming pearl necklace, and matching earrings.

Cerise hoped Santa would find her desirable. It would make things so much easier. She approached him with what she trusted was a casual, confident stroll, watched his round face, and smiled when she caught his eye. The jingling of his bell faltered, and he smiled. His cheeks and nose were rosy from the cold. She ached to touch the lush white beard. His blue eyes twinkled, giving her the confidence to continue.

"Hi," she said as the coins drifted from her sweaty palm into the bucket.

Santa nodded. "Happy holidays," he replied, his gruff voice sending goosebumps down her arms. He cocked his head and flashed her a smile. "Have you been naughty or nice, young lady?"

Cerise froze, her questioning eyes searching Santa's face. Was he flirting with her? Or was it just wishful thinking? She coughed, clearing her throat. "Oh, I've been very, very good, Santa...." She hesitated, and then went on, "But I want so much to be naughty." Cerise's heart beat heavily against her ribs. Would he continue? Or back away?

Santa's eyes brightened, the blue sparkling like jeweled glass ornaments. "How would you like to be Santa's naughty little helper?" He brushed his black-gloved hands over the front of his red velvet pants. "I've got a present with your name on it. Do you want to play with it?"

White-hot fire flashed through her body. Her pussy swelled. She pressed her thighs together, her body pulsing with anticipation. "Yes," she replied, dragging the single word out of her mouth. She couldn't think of anything clever to say. Her mind was going wild. She couldn't concentrate.

Santa jerked his head toward the thick rows of evergreens that leaned up against the shopping center's concrete wall. "Meet me behind those Christmas trees. I need to put the money bucket away before I take my break."

Cerise could only nod. She turned and walked briskly to the trees, not even looking around before stepping behind the curtain of pine needles. The rough walls snagged at her fur, but Cerise didn't care. Her shoes scuffed the brown pine needles on the ground. Setting down her purse, she inspected her surroundings. There was almost enough room for two people, but it was going to be a snug fit.

The freezing breeze softly whistled through the fragrant trees. Cerise inhaled the evergreen scent as the dark grew denser. Then Santa appeared, his bulky figure rustling through the greenery. He moved in front of her, placing his hands on either side of her head. Cerise looked into his eyes, unable to believe her luck. This Santa didn't seem to find her strange. He didn't question her interest, he merely matched her lust, an acceptance that freed her from all sense of inhibition.

She flipped open her fur coat. Her pink nipples puckered as they came into contact with the biting cold. Santa smiled wickedly and lowered his snowy white head. Cerise swallowed hard when he clamped his warm mouth on one nipple; it melted like candy. He pinched its twin, his black woolen glove rough and scratchy. She leaned her head back against the wall and crammed her hands into his white hair, nails scraping slightly over the bald spot as his cap fell onto the frozen ground.

Santa sucked and chewed her nipples as if they were Christmas candy. His cottony-soft beard brushed against her superheated skin as Cerise moaned and spread her shaking legs. She wanted to be totally open and vulnerable to him. To Santa.

His squeezing fingers left her breasts and sought her wet mound. He grabbed her cunt, his abrasive glove tangling with her pubic hair, making her even wetter. Her pelvis bucked, and she rubbed harder against his hand, already close to orgasm. It was much too soon. If this was going to be her last time, Cerise wanted it to last as long as possible. Most of all, she wanted Santa's cock inside her when she came.

"I want to suck you," she pleaded, her voice trembling.

Santa placed his hands on her hips. His breathing was labored and she could smell the scent of her musk. "Unwrap your present, then," he ordered, his eyes shining.

Cerise lowered herself, dead pine needles prickling her bare knees. She enjoyed Santa's playfulness. It made it seem less an obsession than a pastime—something you might even see in a kinky version of *Martha Stewart Living*. Giddy, Cerise imagined herself in a tasteful little photo spread as Santa's very special little helper, maybe in a little green elf-skirt that barely covered her ass. The fantasy was tantalizing.

Cerise pulled down his elastic waistband, crushing the red velvet with her fists. Santa wore bright-red long johns that emphasized the roll of fat at his hips. She wanted to squeeze and mold Santa's malleable body, but she knew she'd come for sure if she did, so she forced herself to shift her attention from Santa's beautiful pudginess and concentrate on his pulsating cock. Placing her cold lips on the tip of his still-thickening penis, she lapped at the pre-cum that appeared. Santa let out a guttural groan and surged into her moist mouth. He clamped his hands on her hair and started thrusting, moaning as the slick heat of her mouth tingled his skin.

His tempo increased as Cerise sucked harder. She fondled his balls with her hands, teasing. He was big, filling her mouth almost to the point of discomfort. But it wasn't her mouth that she really wanted filled. She pulled her head away. "Fuck me now, Santa."

Santa grabbed her by the armpits and pulled her up. He pushed her against the wall, her naked body cushioned by her fur coat. She widened her legs, and he slid between, cock poised to enter. Then he slammed into her cunt, and they both had to muffle their cries.

Santa's gloved hands ran over her naked legs, and then cupped her ass. Cerise arched into him and surrounded his wide girth with her legs. She squeezed her knees into his sides, as Santa hammered into her.

Cerise's orgasm started to gather, quickly gaining power. Her breasts rubbed against the velvety richness of Santa's coat as his wide belt buckle dug into her tender stomach. The fur trim of his jacket tormented the backs of her thighs as she wrapped them around his waist. Threads of desire pulled at all points of her body, gathering in her cunt. Her swollen clit tightened as Santa jerked with his orgasm. His body spasmed violently, mashing Cerise into the building.

She opened her mouth to scream but no sound came. Her body convulsed and she gasped for air. She went limp, shuddering sporadically from the aftershocks.

She leaned against the wall, Santa's weight pressed against her, warm and cuddly. Cerise felt at peace, completely fulfilled from the wild mating. The last Santa had been the best. He was the only one who'd been playful, who'd thought she was fun rather than a freak. This was definitely the perfect time to stop.

"My break is over," Santa murmured against her neck, rubbing his face against her warm pearl necklace. He pushed himself away from her. "I've been waiting for you all season. Started thinking you were a myth. Definitely worth the wait," he said with a wink, sliding out of her.

Cerise frowned, puzzled. "You were waiting for me? I don't understand."

"All of us Santas are from the same company. Kind of like Central Casting. We talk. The guys who've met you all brag about their adventures with 'Santa's Horny Helper.'"

"Santa's Horny Helper?" Cerise pulled her fur coat closed, her sensitive skin still craving his body heat.

Santa shrugged. "Campy, I know, but we didn't have your name. We just know about the pearls and fur. And that you fuck Santas."

Cerise blushed from her toes to her forehead. "And you guys don't think that's weird?"

"Nothing weird about being selective," Santa said as he wiggled up his pants. "Could be worse."

Cerise smiled. She liked Santa's attitude. Selective. It gave the impression that she was in control. Maybe she was.

"My friend who does the downtown shopping area near Saks is dying to meet you, if you're ever there this December."

"I'll keep that in mind," Cerise said, picking up her purse. No need to tell him this was her last time.

"And I'm here three to seven in the evenings."

"That's good to know. I hope you have a merry Christmas."

"I already did, lady. Merry Christmas to you."

Cerise stepped away from their hiding place and quickly walked to her Lexus. She jumped inside and turned the heat on high, fiddling with the radio until *I Saw Mommy Kissing Santa Claus* came pouring from the speakers.

She grinned and checked the time. The stores would close in a couple of hours, and she really needed to do some Christmas shopping. Her mother had been hinting about that Coach wallet she'd seen downtown. Wasn't the Coach store near Saks? She thought it was. She could just nip across town and check.

No! Her mind screamed to a stop. This was her last time. But she *did* need to find something for her mother. And that Santa was looking forward to meeting her. Maybe she should just say hello, she thought, putting the car into gear. Perhaps a little peck on the cheek. It didn't seem right, somehow, for *Santa* not to get what he wanted for Christmas.

JACK'S PRIDE

Emma Holly

I WAS PROUDER OF BUYING THAT BED THAN anything I'd ever done—including marrying Jack, which was no mean feat, what with everyone and her sister trying to chase the poor man to the altar. I bought it with my paycheck from the factory, the factory I'd worked in since the local boys went off to fight the Krauts. The best part was that I bought it after I'd paid the bills, after I'd put my weekly two bucks into Barbara's college fund.

The headpiece was solid brass and curved like a woman's breast. The design wasn't fussy, just graceful, serene. Each time I polished it, I thought: soon. Soon Jack will be home. Soon we'll sleep in this bed together. Each twist of the cloth was a prayer. Bring him back safe, Lord, so that I can show him this beautiful bed, so that I can prove I was braver than anyone—

myself included—ever dreamed I could be.

My heart was in my throat the day Jack came home, with his freshly pressed uniform and his ragged duffel, even quieter than he'd been before, even handsomer, despite the shadows in his eyes. Everything will be all right, I told myself. As soon as he sees the bed.

But Jack didn't like the bed. He didn't say so, of course. Jack wasn't like other men. He didn't yell or hit or get drunk. Jack was like that rock in England, that Gibraltar. But I knew from the dismay in his face that I'd made a terrible mistake.

The world had changed around him. He'd seen buddies blown apart before his eyes. His shy little wife had taken a job. His daughter barely remembered his name. And now I'd taken our sturdy old bed, the bed in which we'd lost our virginity, and I'd replaced it with this shiny, metal cage. I understood his feelings, of course, but, oh, how it hurt! I'd wanted so badly for him to be proud.

But what could I do? Crying wouldn't help. And I couldn't give the bed back. So I went to Bootsie, my partner on the production line—loud Bootsie, brassy Bootsie, who knew more about sex than I would ever dare to learn. Just as I'd suspected, she knew what to do.

I sent Barbara to my mother's and put Grandma's quilt back on the bed, though it had a shredded corner the baby liked to chew when she was teething. I wore my prettiest nightie, the one with the matching peignoir I couldn't pronounce. The gown was silk and it was blue, pale blue, which made my hair look blacker than it is. Jack loved my hair, and I thought I'd take whatever advantage I could get. I dabbed some vanilla between my breasts. I sat. Bing Crosby crooned through the radio, advising me to Accentuate the Positive while I waited for my Jack to come home from work.

My husband had his own auto repair shop outside of town and was getting it running again. It was messy work, but he always showered and shaved before he came home. Still did, though we hadn't made love since his return. Four weeks it had been. Four weeks that seemed longer than the year and a half he'd been away. My cheeks burned as his steady footsteps climbed the stairs. My heart thumped faster than Barbara's when she'd had the croup. Did I dare do what Bootsie said? What if Jack thought I'd lost my mind?

But it was too late to turn back. I switched off the radio and clasped my hands and then Jack was at the door, tall and lean, with his beautiful, serious face and his fresh white T-shirt that always made the place between my legs feel warm and squirmy. Jack has no butt, it's true, but his chest is a sight to behold.

He saw the box first. It was wrapped in gold and topped with a satin bow.

"What's this?" he said.

I handed it to him. "It's a homecoming present. For both of us."

Then he noticed my peignoir. Once upon a time he would have grinned, but tonight he simply raked his hand through his army-short hair, as if the sight of me made him nervous.

"Open it," I said.

He sat on the bed and pried off the lid. The cuffs were on top. His face had no expression as he lifted the velvet ribbons. "What are these?" he said.

I swallowed, but I wouldn't back down. I loved Jack with all my heart. I'd make any sort of fool of myself if I thought it would win him back. "They're for tying your lover to the bed," I said. "Some people like it."

He gave me a funny look. He didn't laugh, though, and he didn't seem angry. Then he took out the paddle.

"Spanking," I said, before he could ask.

This time he did smile, just a little. "Believe me, Rosie," he said. "If I wanted to spank you, I wouldn't need a paddle."

Then something strange happened, something I didn't expect. A flush washed up his neck, like thin red ink spreading beneath the skin. I didn't think I'd ever seen him blush before, not like this, the color so hot I could feel it a foot away.

"You do want to spank me," I gasped. "With your bare hand!"

I shouldn't have been surprised. When it came to men, Bootsie was almost always right. She'd said Jack needed to feel like the boss again. But this was my steady, feet-on-the-ground husband. The thought that he wanted to do this made me quiver with excitement deep inside.

He didn't respond, just reached into the tissue for what was left. He found a tube of lubricating jelly. We'd never used this before because I'd never had trouble getting wet, not even on our wedding night when, truth be told, Jack was more nervous than me. Back then he'd call me his honey pot, and just the words could make me melt. He bounced the tube on his palm and shot a question from under his brows.

Now it was my turn to blush. "It's for...it's for if you wanted to go in the back way."

"The back way?" The corners of his mouth twitched. I was almost sure he was teasing.

"You know. After you'd warmed me up with the paddle."

"Rosie, Rosie, Rosie," he said, but he grabbed me and kissed me, harder than he used to, with his tongue reaching deep and his hands clutching my bottom so that I could tell how excited he was.

Oh, I was so happy to feel that hard, hot ridge, to be able to squirm against his hips and have him moan his longing down my throat. I drove my hands under his clean white T-shirt, greedy to stroke the satiny skin of his back, the tight strong muscles, the long sloping spine.

He kissed me until I couldn't breathe and then he pushed me away. "Climb onto the bed," he said, stern but kind, like a schoolteacher you love but don't dare argue with.

My knees shook as I obeyed.

"Face down," he said, this order sharper than the last. "Put the pillow under your hips and grip the headboard with your hands."

He tied my wrists to the bars with the velvet cuffs and then stepped back. I heard him toeing off his shoes and dropping his pants. I heard the whoosh of cotton as he pulled the T-shirt over his head. I couldn't resist. I had to turn to see him.

He was a sculptor's dream of arms and belly and legs. His penis thrust from his thatch like the staff of life. It was thick and dark. Its head gleamed with seeping tears. His blood pounded through it until it shook like my hands were shaking, like my soul was shaking. I wanted to take him in my mouth and kiss him. I wanted to curl at his feet and weep.

"Did I say you could look?" he demanded.

I shook my head, but didn't turn away. How could I? I wanted to be punished, for the hurts I'd never meant to give him, for the burdens the world had put on his broad young shoulders.

His jaw hardened and he climbed onto the bed behind me. He spread my legs and knelt between them. My bottom was lifted by the pillow. He put one hand on each cheek, lulling me with his warmth. Then he pushed the peignoir up my thighs. Up it went, up, until a draft brushed my curls. He touched them with his thumbs, curling inward through my folds, measuring the sticky flow of my arousal. I could hear him breathing, slow and deep, as if he was trying to control himself but couldn't quite. He caressed my bottom with his palm.

"You need this," he said.

It wasn't a question, but I nodded.

He inhaled deeply, blew out the air, and then he struck. The sting brought tears to my eyes, but I didn't cry out. Again he spanked me and again, scattering the blows across my jiggling curves. A tingle spread through my flesh, a warmth like pepper, a humming like a hive of bees. My sex felt achy and empty, and each blow fed my need. It was a pleasure to want him this badly, but I didn't know how much more I could stand.

"I can't..." he said, the words a cry. I thought he meant he couldn't go on, but he grabbed the tube of jelly that had fallen onto the bed.

Oh, I thought, my body tightening with anticipation. Oh, yes.

He didn't scold me when I turned to watch him squeeze the lubricant down his shaft. His hands were trembling, his balls drawn up like two spring plums. He couldn't wait. That's what he'd meant: that he couldn't wait to get inside. Excitement swept through my veins in hot, drunken waves.

"I want you," I said, ragged as smoke. "I want to give you everything I have."

His face darkened. A pulse beat visibly in his neck. He pulled me onto my knees, roughly, growling like an animal when my bottom hit his groin. He split my cheeks between his thumbs. He pressed his swollen crown against the star of my secret hole. "I'm going to take it," he said, and I could barely understand the words. "I'm going to take you."

He pressed against my body's resistance, pressed until it hurt like our wedding night. Like then, the snap of pain lasted only a moment. Pleasure followed, immense, shattering. He conquered my body and my fears. The throb of him was lovely, the heat and hardness, the living, quaking silk. His sigh warmed my neck as he folded down around me. His hand cupped my mound of Venus. His fingers found my pleasure's heart. With a moan of long-denied delight, he drew back and thrust.

Slow and steady he drove us, up toward bliss, up toward daylight. I whimpered as he held me on the edge and felt his teeth nip the skin of my nape.

"Come," he said and pinched the tender button of my sex.

I came like an orange bursting in the sun. I came dripping and crying and shuddering with sweetness. He pushed two fingers inside me, throwing me over again, and then followed with a heavy, jolting thrust. I felt the spasms of his seed. His groan mixed with grief and joy in one.

"Good girl," he said as we lay in a heap, my head on his shoulder, his hand petting my tangled hair. "You're the best wife a husband could have."

He was proud of me after all.

KALI

Maryanne Mohanraj

SO YOU'RE WALKING UP AND DOWN TELEGRAPH
Avenue, up and down, trying not to look like
the new dyke in town, trying not to broadcast
that you're fresh off the boat, innocent new
meat just in from Indiana, come to the big city.
Actually, the small city—to Berkeley in fact,
because San Francisco is a little intimidating to
start off with if you're a 22-year-old dyke who
came all the way to California to get laid
because you've been dumped by the only other
lesbian in Franklin, Indiana, and you just can't
take it any more.

The women certainly are pretty, in Berkeley,
in the springtime. Campus chicks in blue jeans
and T-shirts and bandannas; skin in shades
you've never seen on a TV set. Lots of skin—
they don't seem to feel the cold that's prickling
your skin. You are determined not to pull the

sweatshirt out of your backpack, not to shiver in this dark-green tank top with the scoop neck that shows your ample cleavage for the benefit of any cute chick who might happen to like tall redheads who probably still look like farm girls.

You've been cruising Berkeley for weeks now. Days working over on Shattuck, over at the games store whose owners seemed surprised to have a woman actually want the job. Boys and their toys! Evenings on the street, up and down, occasionally smiling at a woman with short dark hair and long legs, the kind of legs that could reach back and wrap all the way around your neck as you bump and grind, oh yes. Smiling at her and she smiles back and your heart does the thump-thing and then she keeps going down the street, or asks you if you have the time and then keeps going and you're back to walking the street again wondering where the hell women go to get laid in this town.

Up past the hippie chicks, up past the man who tries to sell you beads for your hair at three times what it would cost in Franklin, all the way up to the campus, turn and start walking down again. Maybe it's time to get up the nerve to go into San Francisco, find one of those girl-gyms, those dyke-diners you keep hearing about, uh-huh. You walk down past Cody's Bookstore, hover in the window of the poster shop, scope out the new new-age books at Shambhala.

It sure would be a lot easier to walk into one of those diners with a beautiful woman on your arm, a pretty little thing like that dark-skinned girl behind the counter, the one with the long black hair braided down her back, with the tight white shirt that outlines breasts the size of softballs, the one walking over to take something out of a window, the one smiling at you through the glass. Right. And now she's going to turn away or come to the door and ask if you wanted to actually buy anything or were just planning to hang out there and scare away the customers. You brace yourself, and then she stares at you real serious, and then she winks. Long and slow, and you can't believe what you're seeing, and you check to make sure you've got your pink triangle earring in where she can see it and oh yes, it's there, and then she's coming to the door and it's "I get off in 15 minutes. Want to buy me coffee?" and you are stumbling over yourself to say yes.

Fifteen minutes and the coffee shop and her name all slide by in a blur—you've forgotten her name but you can't admit it, so you just keep smiling and hope and pray that she doesn't think you're a total twit, a ditz, a baby dyke without a clue. After coffee you're walking down the street and you tell her all about your last relationship and how bad it went, doing your damnedest to convince her of your dyke credentials until she grins and says, "Hush—now is not the time" and then she pulls you into a doorway and starts kissing you. She is at least a foot shorter than you, but she's up on her toes and pulling you down with no hesitation and the kissing is easy, so easy and hot you're melting into it, and then the door you're leaning on starts to open and you realize that her hand is on the doorknob and her key is in the door and this is, of course, the door to her apartment and she's taking you upstairs, woohoo!

She kisses you all the way up three flights of stairs, and her hands are all over you, over the T-shirt, under the T-shirt, under your bra to cup your breasts, squeeze your nipples, pull you up the last steps with her fingers tight on your nipples and her mouth latched to yours, and you are tumbling into her apartment and closing the door with your bodies 'cause your hands are too damn busy to spare. She breaks long enough to turn on the light and fire up some candles and incense and turn off the light again and then you are falling to the futon in the living room, lit by candles, the room is full of candles and statues and flowers and incense. You're a little dizzy, but when she pulls off your shirt and bra and starts licking a nipple you have to know, you say, "Hang on," and "I hate to ask this" and "What's your name again?" and wait for her to throw you out.

She laughs instead, and says, "Kali; my name is Kali," and then she gets this wide grin and lies back on the futon and says, "Kali is a goddess, you know? Worship me."

You've never touched a goddess before, but your mama didn't raise no fools, and so you get her and you out of clothes as fast as you can, before she has a chance to take a proper breath or change her mind, and then you're kissing her. Sucking on her toes and calves and knees and thighs, up around her clit, up her curving stomach and softball breasts, down to fingers and up again, kissing and sucking and licking until your mouth is dry and her skin is wet and shaking in the wavering light of what seem a hundred candles.

You worship her with mouth and hands, you slide a finger in her cunt and then another until they are slick and salty, and you bring them up to your mouth and taste them, lick them with Kali's eyes on you, glittering, and she breathes "More," and you go down, you breathe on, lick, and suck her clit, slide two fingers in again, thrust back and forth and she is writhing beneath you, she is silent but her body speaks. It whispers and moans and whimpers and screams and she is almost there and you can't quite do it, you can't get her there, you can feel the crest waiting there, the last lap, the last mile, and you're not going to make it, you're not good enough and you are ready to lay your head down on her stomach and cry if she will permit it.

You stop, removing the once-thrusting, now-sore fingers. She whimpers, and your stomach churns, and you take a deep, gasping breath. Kali opens her eyes then and sees you and she is not angry. She is twisted in on herself, she is bathed in sweat, dripping in the candlelight, and she says, "It's OK" and takes a deep breath and you can see that she is going to try to come down, to relax, to let it go and, dammit, that is not good enough, you know you can do better than this—and then inspiration hits. You slide back down, your mouth is on her again, on that sweet-salty mound, on that wet nubbin, and while you lick and she convulses silently again, starting the climb again, your hand reaches out and grabs a candle.

Your eyes are closed against her skin but you can feel the slim, cool shape of it, bubbled with old dripped wax, long and hard and untiring. You wave it in the air to put it out, you wait for it to cool as your tongue tickles and touches, twisting to penetrate every crevice, every inch it can reach, and when it is exhausted, when it feels that it is about to break in two, to shatter into a thousand pieces, that is when you reverse the shape in your hand and slide it into her, into her dripping cavity, sliding it smooth and hard into her, and Kali gasps beneath you and her hands come down to your shoulders, her fingers dig into your skin, and you know that you guessed right. You push and pull, thrusting hard and fast until finally, finally her back arches, her hips convulse, and she freezes still and silent for an endless, aching time, and even if your fingers and tongue fall off you are not going to move one inch in the wrong direction. And then she relaxes.

She pulls you up, after a time, and you make love in all the clever ways that two young dykes in the prime of their strength and stamina can, and she discovers how easily you come, how even nipple-sucking can do it, and she says that she might forgive you for that someday. Hours pass, and the candles are long burned out, and you are settling down to sleep but can't quite get comfortable, there's a lump, a bump in the sheets under your hip, and you realize that you've left the candle there and are surprised it's still in one piece and you reach down and pull it out and in the thin moonlight you realize that it isn't a candle after all.

A statue of a goddess, a naked goddess, and the bumps you took for dripping candle wax are breasts and curved hands, many hands, and you catch your breath, wondering if you have committed some form of sacrilege, if Kali will recoil in shock, horror, dismay, and she must see it in your eyes because she laughs and laughs and eventually, gently, explains that she is not religious, definitely not Hindu, that her family was in fact Catholic.

She herself had turned atheist long ago, she says, and got the statues from the new-age bookstore free. She tells you that she only keeps them around 'cause they're pretty and they seem to turn on the chicks, and you blush and are grateful for the thinness of the light. She also says that even if she did believe in the goddess, she doesn't think She would mind being deep inside a woman's wet cunt. Then she confesses a secret—that Kali is only her work name, after all, that it impresses the bookstore clients. Her true name is something she takes seriously, and she never tells it to lovers unless they stay around long enough for breakfast. And when you get over being embarrassed and amused and slightly shocked, you tell her that you think you could probably arrange that.

MY KIND OF WOMAN

J.L. Belrose

WHEN I GET STUCK IN A DRY SPELL, I SHUFFLE the deck real good to see what'll come up. That's why, not quite desperate but definitely needy, I'm outside Lola's.

Lola's isn't my kind of place. I like comfortable, almost shabby lesbian bars where people kick back, and where there are usually one or two washroom cubicles with broken locks that somehow never get fixed. But Lola's is a prissy place, all fancy exposed brickwork and pencil sketches and stained glass. And so many mirrored walls in three interconnected rooms that a person has to be careful not to walk into one, or even worse, cruise herself. As for the washrooms, they're so pristine that taking a piss there feels more like a medical procedure than a social opportunity.

Lola's attracts an eclectic, gender-mixed,

affluent crowd of hets and queers and trannies and bi's. Which is OK by me. There's space enough in my universe for everyone. But the truth is, when it comes to scratching my itch, I have an extremely narrow focus: women. More specifically, butch women. The kick-ass kind. The kind who've been around the block a few times and are proud of their scars. But, as I said, things seem as stale as reheated coffee at the two lezzie bars in town, and I need a jolt of espresso. Lola's, I figure, is worth checking out.

I make my entrance. I'm dressed for the occasion, as cool and polished as smoked-glass and chrome, in my black vinyl miniskirt, red silk slip-top, and silver "come-fuck-me" shoes. I match my leggy stride to the wide shallow steps that descend between ornate wrought iron railings from street level down into Lola's main bar. I scan the roomful of glam dresses and preppy-boy suits and ties. Quick cruise, then outta here, I instruct myself. But one woman snags my attention.

She's standing, facing the stairs, propped against one of the square brick pillars that divide the main room from the back ones. Positioned the way she is to see everyone coming in, I'm sure she watched my stagey lope down the stairs. I slow down, make a smooth left, and head for a spot at the bar where I can perch for a moment and check her out.

I dub her The Cowboy. She isn't my type, except that she's big. I do like big women. She's all in denim, with a wide-brimmed black hat tipped forward, almost obscuring her eyes. Maybe that's what attracts me—her aura of mystery. What turns me off, though, is the hair. She has long black hair frizzing from hat to shoulders. "Do yourself a favor, doll. Get a barber," I mutter.

I decide to do the other rooms. To do so I must pass The Cowboy, but, so that she won't think I'm cruising her, I focus elsewhere. Only when I'm almost past her do I sneak an approving glance at her belly. That's when I see the bulge down the inside of her right leg. For a nanosecond I'm immobilized by the buzz from my cunt, but then I move on. As I said, she's not really my type. Nothing in the other two rooms slows me down. I read het sightseers, maybe swingers, maybe bi-curious, mixed in with the usual clientele. Not my kind of crowd. And, judging by the music, it's a Spanish theme night. Not my kind of music either. "I'm outta here," I say.

A drag queen, dazzling in red sequins, strikes a startled pose and observes me. "Do you always talk to yourself?" she inquires.

"Yah," I say, "If you're not interested, don't listen."

I pass The Cowboy again on the way out. Of course, I take another look. I don't know whether her move is deliberate timing or just coincidence, but as I pass, she reaches down and squeezes the bulge. My cunt clenches and I do a classic double take. I change my mind about leaving, veer over to the bar, and anchor my ass to a stool, angling my long legs out sideways. I believe in displaying my assets. Obviously, The Cowboy does too.

I unzip my silver fanny-pack, extract my compact and a five-dollar bill, check my face and hair, and order a Corona. The bottle doesn't reach my mouth before I see The Cowboy bumping around to the music, swaying from side to side, her chin pushed down into her neck, her shoulders humped. "Too weird," I say. I keep watching her, though, embarrassed for her and turned off, yet fascinated.

People start giving her space as if her problem might be contagious. Then her foot paws the floor and, suddenly, it comes together for me. The music's like "Dance of the Toreadors" or something, and she's enacting a bullfight, but really she's thumbing her nose at the establishment, the music, maybe at everything. I can relate. I can respect her. It takes balls to make that kind of statement in a PC place like Lola's. I tip my bottle, get the last trickle of beer, and slide off my stool.

Her head is down. She's deep into her dance. I don't think she sees me stride over, but she doesn't seem surprised when she looks up and I'm posed, legs spread, hands on my hips, in front of her. "Honey," I say, "You need a matador, and I'm the girl for it." I motion to the back room, which I know is almost empty, and walk away. I don't have to look back to know she's behind me, feet shuffling, arms pumping, a conga line of one. I put an extra wiggle on my ass, leading her on.

As soon as we're more secluded, I pivot to face her. I pull off my top. I'm pleased with myself for not wearing a bra. My nipples are pointy in their rings. I flutter my red silk-top at my side like a cape. Her "charge" is a cha-cha, which she continues in a full circle around me. She stops in front of me, unbuttons her jeans, unzips her fly, and hauls out a large cock. It's one of those realistic units, with a bulbous head and engorged veins.

She resumes her dance. Her jeans slide down on her hips, and the cock bounces around freer and freer between her legs. The few people who were in the room have moved back to form a loose circle around us. More people are coming in, but I don't care. I can't take my eyes off the cock. I want so bad to suck it. My "cape" falls from my hands, and I go down on my knees. With my eyes, I beg her to dance closer. I want to stretch my lips around the ridged head, tease its pee-hole with my tongue. I want to suck and swallow, flatten my tongue under the veined shaft, take it in till it hurts. Till my throat screams. Till I choke, face streaming tears.

But our scene is abruptly shattered. It sags under a collective groan as Tony, the manager, shrieking "Ladies! Ladies! Ladies!" in mounting hysteria, pushes through the crowd. "We can't allow this. No! No! No! This is not allowed," he jabbers, amid groans that turn into boos. He flaps around, looking like a nervous penguin in his black suit. The spectators clearly want the show to continue.

Suspended in some kind of limbo, I can't move. I watch with plunging disappointment as The Cowboy stuffs her cock back into her jeans and struggles with the zipper. Then someone shoves Tony and he pleads, "Let's everyone calm down. We don't want the cops now, do we?"

The red-sequined drag queen bats his arm with her purse. "They were dancing," she informs him, using her superior height to full advantage. "Are there laws against dancing?" My arms are seized from behind, and I'm hauled to my feet by The Cowboy. "Come on," she says and propels me toward an emergency exit and up some stairs. "I've been here before. It gets crazy."

As the door closes behind us I hear a distant tinkle of breaking glass, but I'm totally distracted from what's happening inside when The Cowboy yanks off her hat and her hair comes off with it. "What?" I stammer. It turns into "Wow!" as I focus on a short bristle of silver hair. My brain flashes neon at my cunt. My kind of woman! The small silver rings on each of her eyebrows and down both her ears make her perfect. Just looking at her makes me gush.

I guess she feels she has to explain. "There's been trouble before when I've been here," she says. "It wasn't my fault, but I don't get past the door any more if Tony recognizes me. They're crazy. Tony's a prick."

"Shit happens," I say, and shrug. The trouble that comes to my kind of women is never their fault. At least, that's how they tell it. And, truth is, I don't care. I love them anyway, whatever kind of hard-luck jams they get into.

She leads me through the alley beside the building until we come to a high wooden fence. The boards are thin; when she puts her boot to the flimsy gate it falls apart. I follow her into a deserted patio where round wooden picnic tables squat in the shadows, and tubs of dead plants display ghost-flowers in the moonlight. "We're OK here," she assures me, settling her butt onto the edge of a table in a dark corner near the building. She folds her arms across her chest and waits for me to make the next move.

I don't disappoint her. I toss my top on the table beside her hat and wig. Then I unzip my fanny-pack and come up with a rubber and lube. The lopsided smirk she gives me is exactly what I expect from her. "I love girls who come prepared," she says "and know what they want."

Fingers of cool night air caress my bare back. I don't know whether I'm shivering or trembling in anticipation as she undoes her jeans and exposes her cock. I want to mount her. I think how awesomely depraved I would feel, climbing onto her as she sits against the table. I imagine grasping her cock, positioning the head in my cunt, and then pushing myself down onto it. Then I wonder if I wouldn't rather present my ass to her. I imagine the exquisite stretching and fullness. I decide there's no reason I shouldn't get it both ways. But muffled voices and shuffling sounds come from the alley between the buildings. I hesitate. How long, I wonder, before someone notices the broken gate?

I tear at the small foil square. "We don't have much time," I say. She sighs agreement and steadies her dick while I bag it.

Louder voices poke peepholes through the wall of fence and dark surrounding us. A siren, muted by distance, disturbs the mumble of city noise. My skin prickles with excitement. She shoves off the table. "Lean over," she says, indicating where she'd been sitting.

I obey, not unhappy she's made the decision for me. She lifts my skirt and turns it up over my back, strokes up the inside of my thigh, and then runs a finger teasingly under the edge of my panty leg. "You OK with this?" she asks.

"Yes," I say, so horny I almost dance.

She hooks her fingers into the waist of my panties, pulls them off over my ass, and pushes them down my legs until they slip the rest of the way to my feet. I free one foot and spread my legs. The voices sound angry, but seem as if they're further away, out on the street, in front of the building. Someone is shouting about living in a "free fucking country" and a higher octave, maybe Tony, shrieks about "private property."

She eases a lubed finger into my asshole. I wait as she smears her cock. Neither one of us suggests stopping, or going anywhere safer. It's as if our hearts are beating in tandem and our minds are in sync, and I know her need like I know my own. We like the edge, the danger. She tests me, her cockhead nudging my asshole. I breathe evenly and fog my mind with an image of loosening, accepting the shaft. Slowly, she slides in. I grunt with satisfaction, the fullness almost unbearable.

A crash of glass riffs through the night. I tingle as if a thousand tiny splinters have embedded themselves in my spine. If The Cowboy hears it, it doesn't interrupt her. She reaches an arm around and pushes her hand between my legs from the front. Her fingers find my clit, then my cunt hole, and push their way into the compressed space. "Oh, yes. Oh, yes," I chant, begging for more, knowing I can't take more. I'm full of her. Too full.

Sirens scream as if they're coming in on top of us. Maybe I scream too as I clutch at an orgasm. She groans as she strokes my clit, giving me my last throbs of pleasure. Then, gently, she pulls out. I'm empty. I straighten up and lean back against her. For just a moment, her forehead rests on my shoulder. "I'm sorry, sweetie," she rasps into my neck. "I'm gonna hafta bail. There's gonna be cops around."

"It's OK," I say.

"I've been in trouble before."

"Yah, it's OK," I tell her. "Go." My kind of women are always on the run. They arrive late, and leave early. And, truth is, I like it that way. It doesn't get complicated, and it's never boring.

She tosses the rubber and is still doing herself up as she moves off into the darkness. I pull up my panties, smooth down my skirt, slip on my top, and stand for a minute in the dark against the building. I know there's a back way out of the patio because The Cowboy has disappeared that way, but I decide not to risk breaking an ankle in a dark back lane. Besides, strutting out the front way, with an I've-been-fucked smile on my face, reveling in the sweet discomfort in my ass, is more my style.

There's a cop car parked in the street, but the cops must be in Lola's. Most of the front window lies in shards on the sidewalk. A few people are standing around, curious but keeping a distance, not looking to get involved. I blow an air-kiss through the hole in the window. "Thanks," I say to Lola's. "Bye, now." I have no plans to return. As I said, it's not my kind of place.

But Saturday comes around again and I decide to go back. I can't kick The Cowboy out of my mind. And, fact is, we didn't really have enough time. "Unfinished business," you could say. I hate unfinished business.

The window's been repaired, and the place looks as prissily perfect as ever, as if the past weekend hadn't happened. I'd be doubting my sanity if my ass didn't have its own set of memory cells. I scan the room from the top of the stairs. It's much the same crowd, except there's no Cowboy leaning against the pillar. I shrug, disappointed. I'm turning to leave when I spot a big woman at the end of the bar. She's wearing a jacket that, with all its brass buttons, looks like a costume piece from a military pageant. She has a mass of curly red hair, and the visor of her cap is pulled down over her eyes.

I redub her The General and decide to march up to her, salute smartly, and get my orders. But I don't get to the bottom of the stairs before Tony zooms in out of nowhere like a heat-seeking missile. "We don't want more trouble," he blusters. "You have to leave."

I give him my amazon-queen stare, but he hangs there, looking like a pugnacious parrot in his green suit. "Listen, darling," I say, "I don't know what happened, but it wasn't my fault. OK?"

There is, however, no reasoning with him. I glance toward
The General. She hasn't moved. I can see she's not going to: it's
obviously every man for himself on this battlefield. I retreat
while my grace and dignity are intact. I hang around outside for
a few minutes, thinking she might come out to reconnoiter her
troops, but she doesn't. "Piss on this," I say, and stomp off.

I fume for days. I go to sleep every night masturbating, plot-
ting revenge. I hate being foiled—it's like rope burn across my
breast. Suddenly, I realize I'm being stupid. I'm at work, in the
middle of taking an order, when I get my enlightenment.
"Eureka!" I say, and know what to do.

I'm ready when the weekend comes, and I'm dapper as hell
when I walk into Lola's. My hair's jelled back, except for a few
strands falling casually across my forehead. I get a glimpse of
myself in the mirrored wall and am amazed by the tall young
man I see. It's incredible what professionally applied facial hair
can do for a girl.

My breasts are flattened by an undershirt two sizes too
small, and I'm sporting a three-piece suit, tie, and wing tips.
I've got the moves down, too. I slouch down the stairs, hands
in my pockets, swagger across the room, and pose at the bar.
And, OK, I know it's twisted, but I cruise Tony. Just for the hell
of it.

I'm somewhat unnerved when he puffs up as if maybe he's
interested. I smile because it's so damn funny, but it must be the
right kind of smile for him. He holds me in a long bold stare,
and then flicks his eyes toward the john. The invitation is
unmistakable. I drop my eyelids in a way that, I hope, signifies
indolent rejection. Then I move on. I figure we're even.

My real interest, of course, is the big woman standing with
her back against the wall near the foot of the stairs. She's checking out everyone coming in, but I'm sure she didn't pay much
attention to me. If I didn't know better, I'd say she wasn't my
type. She has stringy brown hair hanging lankly around her

face, and a baseball cap pulled down over her eyes. She's wearing some kind of team jacket. I redub her The Jock.

I lean, elbows back, against the bar and stare at her until she finally glares back. That's my cue. I step forward, wind up, and pitch an imaginary ball in her direction. She scowls at me and turns away. But it's not long before she's checking me out again. I wind up for another pitch. Then another. She's so nonplussed she just stands there, and takes the third strike.

I make my walk in to the plate. She slams me with a stony look that makes me hope she isn't going to haul back and slug me. I adjust my crotch. "Excuse me," I say, "This team needs a switch-hitter, and I'm your girl."

"Fuck!" she splutters, as my voice puts it together for her. She reaches out and gingerly touches my beard. "Fuck!" she says again, and chuckles. "I guess this one's going to be a doubleheader."

"Yup," I say, leading the way to the dugout, which happens to be in Lola's washroom. As I said, she's my kind of woman.

SÉVERINE

Hanne Blank

IT PAINED HER TO BE SO FAR AWAY. PARIS LURKED obstinately on another side of the globe, no matter how hard she shut her eyes and imagined the lights from the rooftop where they used to sit and smoke, just the two of them.

Alain did not like it when she sat on the stone rim of the roof, furrows in his high forehead betraying his fear of heights. He never ventured to the ledge, but sat with his back against the chimney-pot, talking with Séverine as she watched the city the way a sailor's wife watches the sea. The pre-bedtime cigarette on the roof was their ritual, regardless of season, and not merely because they didn't dare smoke indoors. If they did, Marie-Sophie would pout and shut herself away in her room like a petulant schoolgirl. It hurt her lungs, she said, which a singer should not countenance.

Marie-Sophie: such a little prima donna, such gorgeous platinum ringlets, such sweet plump lips. At both ends, oh yes, and juicy like a plum of soft ivory, ripe under the teeth. But such a brat! I am not immune to her, though. None of us is, no matter what she does. Sophie is *un feu d'artifice,* our silver baby, the maddening dragonfly that buzzes around our heads when we try to be serious. She drives Alain crazy, to the point that he screams, and then leaves for a day or two, which shouldn't make me panic but always does. And yet we all struggled to seduce her to stay, didn't we? Especially Alain. He tried and failed to push her out of his heart, he said, and so he simply had had to learn to let her have her way. We should all be so impossible not to love.

Séverine ground out her cigarette on the windowsill bricks, exhaling long and slow into the velvet humidity of the Vancouver afternoon. Four months until the contract was up, just four more.

She could remember them at that hour, sleep noises drifting through the high-ceilinged spaces of the old row house. There would be Marie-Sophie and Alain, curled into one another in Alain's room at the top of the stairs, at least until Marie-Sophie crept back downstairs to Corinne's side, taking refuge from the snoring. Corinne would murmur and shift in her sleep, unruffled, pressing closer to Séverine as she unconsciously made room for the peripatetic Marie-Sophie. In the morning Corinne's smile was like the sun itself, broadcasting delight at once more finding herself surrounded by the people she loved best. Some mornings Alain would fumble down the stairs, unhappy at having woken up alone, and slip among the three of them, completing the sleepy family beneath the quilts. Later there would be coffee and *pain de campagne* and jam and the ritual bickering over the shower. It was all good, even the tatty, cat-scratched upholstery on the sofa in the front room.

It had been three years, and still Séverine marveled that it had happened at all. She had resisted sharing the house at first. It was too much; it seemed too much risk to shift her foundation so that she had no safety zone, no place to run. But Alain had made her a small yellow room, just beside his own, and had put anemones in the vase beside the window, and soon she had come to stay. It had been her birthday when they kissed her down to her bed, both of them, and baptized her with semen and sweat and welcomed her home. Three years ago, the 16th of February, cold and clear and half a world away.

Impossible to think of Alain without Corinne. By comparison I am merely a satellite, orbiting the gravity of Alain's long fingers and sly humor, the pull of sweet Corinne's thick hips and calm love. Such patience Alain had with me! Corinne is not patient; she simply does what she does and lets what must happen, happen. Same destination, different journeys.

I miss them together and apart. Alain's sardonic jokes, his long skinny cock, the way he strokes into me to make me squeal, and the fact that he loves seeing me in the morning, rumpled and crusted with sleep, so that he can tease me. Corinne's voluptuous cruelties, her heavy hand landing again and again on my pale raised ass, her filthy whispers, her silent generosity and enormous thighs, the depths of her drenched hothouse cunt around my hand, over my face. Her serenity. The madonna with a laptop. Her consort in his suit, official, imposing, slicing through the week with carbon-steel words of law. Impossible to imagine either of them without some reference to the other. Somewhere between them both, they have changed me. I have ceased to exist as I did before. Like the moon the earth's, I require their substance to keep me where I need to be.

Séverine sighed heavily as she pulled her head back inside. Somberly she looked out at Mount Seymour's rain-shrouded flanks, recalling the sounds of Marie-Sophie's sultry giggle over the phone lines, Alain's low-voiced chuckle as he told a joke that he knew would make her blush, Corinne's sweetly stern admonitions that she was not to feel too sorry for herself being alone on her birthday. Perhaps she would wait until it was morning there and call them again.

She stared at the telephone. No, it would not do. Yes, she missed them, but it didn't help to be a baby. Besides, the money on this job was worth it, was it not? She would take them all to Greece for a month when she returned. They would sail, and grill fish over a small fire, and the sounds of water and wind would be quilted with the soft gasps of her lovers, together and separately. At night they would all sit on the terrace and talk, mending the small, inevitable tears in the fabric of a family that come with a member's prolonged absence. In Greece she'd have them again, on a small island of blues and whites and endless, free-roaming cats. Perhaps the travel brochures she had ordered would be in the afternoon mail.

The mailbox door was jammed. The small box was crammed, the outermost layer consisting of three large tan envelopes, bent around the other mail to fit them in. She wriggled them out, catching sight of Corinne's strongly slanted script on the corner of one of them. In large letters across the bottom of the envelope she read *Attention, Photos! Ne pas plier.* Séverine scowled, ironing the envelopes flat with her palm. Weren't Canadian postal workers supposed to be able to read French?

Nonetheless Séverine smiled happily as she ascended the stairs, shuffling the bills to the bottom of the stack and observing, with intensifying excitement, that Corinne, Marie-Sophie, and Alain had each sent something. Birthday cards, she supposed gleefully, happy at the timing of the often undependable international post. Perhaps there would even be letters inside, or photos. Séverine had photos of her three partners elsewhere, of course, but that was not the same as new ones.

Séverine took the letters with her into the bedroom, nudging the shoes from her feet as she leaned back against the pillows. She took Alain's letter first, lifting it to her nose as she opened it. The scent of lilac mingled with black cigarettes brought tears of longing to her eyes. The paper had been folded around something stiff, and as she unfolded the letter, two Polaroids fell onto the bed at her side. She picked them up and gasped softly, as a hot flush crept over her face and down onto her chest, and a similar heat tingled between her legs. Almost unable to believe it, she shook her head and laughed, feeling dazed.

Merde. Photographs. I did not know, but how could I have known? I could not see them, and there was enough noise, between that loud little Mademoiselle of ours and the sound of my pounding heart and hard breathing that I probably didn't hear the camera whir. Even if I had, would I have known? Even had I known, what would I have done? Nothing, nothing. Corinne tied me too tightly for that. The most I could have done was tell them no, beg them to stop. And even that—well. *Mon dieu.* I had not forgotten this—how could I? But to live it again, in the cold light of distance and not with the comforting blur of lust....

So disgusting. So beautiful.

> Séverine, my love,
> You will agree, yes, even you must agree that you are a treasure when you see these photographs. We did not tell you, no, but it was not then your prerogative to know. You had only two duties the night before you flew away—to keep your restless tongue busy, and to open to us as we took our fill of you. We knew that we would miss you too badly to let you leave us less than glutted. And we did have your best interests at heart: you recall that you, a panicky flyer, slept well on the airplane.

I look at these photos, lurid as they are, and remember
only sacredness and love. You, I am sure, do not find that
strange, but you are a benevolent angel of flesh and always
have been. It startles me somewhat to see you at this remove,
here in my hand, as lusciously passive as you were between
my thighs, to see the blissful relaxation on your face as my
cock slid between your lips, deeper and deeper into your
mouth and throat. I can almost feel the awed and grateful
hum as I slowly drove the length of myself against the
tangling swirl of your agile tongue. The grace with which you
receive me belies the ugliness of the name of the act each time
I straddle your head and fuck long and solid.

You have always loved being mouth-fucked that way. Only
Corinne's bites and strong hands make you as wet, as ready,
force you to come as wantonly as does the sensation of my
cock so forcefully invading your elegant mouth.

We all watched you disrobe for us, and when you stood
naked and Marie-Sophie brought your corset, Corinne took
your arms and cuffed them over your head as I stroked your
lovely face. Marie-Sophie laced you in, too tightly, which is to
say just tightly enough. Cori kissed you, do you recall? You
melted against her as she explained to you what you already
knew: that you were ours, that we would take you, each
alone and all together, using your mouth, your cunt, your ass,
your breasts, however it pleased us. You clung to her
desperately, your lips in a crimson circle against her neck, and
my heart leapt impossibly, desperate to keep you with us,
horrified to think of letting you go so far away.

I could not touch you for several moments, the phantom
of impending loss too present, but then they lay you down on
the quilts, in Corinne's room, on the mattresses that cover the
floor, and you looked up at me with curiously childlike eyes.
The other two were busy with you, Marie-Sophie already
kneeling down between your legs, Corinne chaining your

wrists to the wall (not that you would have resisted us), and yet I felt almost as if you had forgotten them. "Please, Alain, you mustn't," you said, your voice soft. "I need you, please, in my mouth so that I can remember how you use me so well. Fuck my mouth, Alain, please?"

Corinne slipped on your eyeshade and I straddled your head facing Marie-Sophie, whose blonde curls bobbed as her wicked tongue teased you. I looked down at your leather-cinched form, your pretty breasts pushed up and out of the corset, wondering whether Marie-Sophie would make you gasp before I could. To my surprise, she did not. As if you had been waiting for me despite the tongue flickering at your submissive clit, it was not until I had sunk myself in your mouth to the hilt that your body finally shuddered and you began to writhe. But then you have said that you never feel so thoroughly caught up in sex as when your mouth is being ruthlessly used, when a cock crushes your lips against your teeth or when you are within a gasp of smothering from the relentless bucking of cunt against your teeth and tongue.

I used you harder than I meant to. The agony of knowing I was to lose you, if only for a time, pushed my hips against your face harder than I should have let them. Oh, I remember it! No one else, no one, takes a cock like you, *belle* Séverine; nothing can compare with the cannibal orchid of your throat. Do you see in this photograph how you lay there, saliva in a stream down your cheek, my cock buried to the hilt in your throat as you took me in, the raw and open vessel of the fuck?

I used you every way I could, so that when you left you would have the essence of me in your belly, in your cunt, in your ass, in your skin where Corinne rubbed our mingled juices into your face and breasts. It seemed crucial, somehow, to be inside each part of you, to leave a trace of myself so that you could find me again.

Look at the photos, *belle hirondelle,* do you see the expression on your face? Here, where I was in your pert ass, Marie-Sophie's hand in you to her slim doll's wrist, Cori's quicksilver all over your face, do you see it? Do you see with what angelic purity you took it, and let us use you? You burned for us, from the inside, a cathedral at Christmas.

Yes, *chérie,* we miss you. I miss you. I smoke in the evenings on the rooftop, alone now but for the notebook and pen I take with me when it is dry and clear. It will please you that I sit on the ledge now, and it will probably please you more that, once in a while, when there is an empty space in the air next to me that is shaped particularly like you, I lay down that old green-gray blanket behind the chimney-pot where we once made love, and I watch the stars and stroke myself and think of you.

Bon anniversaire, Séverine, *mon amour.*

Lying on the bed, Séverine let the hand that held the letter droop to her chest, the paper curling against her breasts. Her small nipples were hard as the points of darts beneath her sweater. At the sight of the photos of herself being so deliciously used, tightly clamped nipples so cruelly pulled toward one another by the short chain that connected the clamps, Alain's cock buried in her throat, her hips had begun to undulate of their own will, pushing her clit toward the seam of her jeans. She could almost taste Corinne's sweet liquor, feel the meaty bulb of her fat clit mashed against her tongue. Séverine slid her hand under the waistband of her jeans, fingers slipping easily between her puffy lips into the sweet sea-water slickness between as she picked up the photos again. Longingly she saw, and remembered, Alain roughly penetrating her bound, helpless body. His cock in her ass, not as thick as the dildo Corinne had forced into her, but longer, so that when he fucked her she felt the forbidden deliciousness in her deepest, most secret of spaces. In the picture, all but a few centimeters were buried in between the smooth halves of her ass, and she scissored her clitoris between her fingers, remembering the time that he had made her count as he worked it into her that way, counting one two three four five, all the way to 24 centimeters before he was buried in her ass to his balls.

Alain! How dare you write to me like this, how dare you send the photographs and not be here to take me that way again! I am here with one hand in my jeans, fingers slick, remembering that night and the taste of you, remembering the sheer, inescapable need each time you lunged into me. Yes, you battered me, you left me bruised. You ground my lips against my teeth so that for a week I looked as if Sophie had sent me off with her bee-stung pout as a parting gift. Your strokes kept me grounded amid the stairways of anguish and delight that rose from Cori's mouth on my nipples, Sophie's on my cunt, the fingers in my pussy, that dildo Corinne drove slowly into my ass to be ready for you (it was too big, it was, and it hurt, but only for an instant and only as it melted into the thick cream of pleasure).

I did not lie. I needed you to fuck my mouth, to make me necessary, to let me give and not merely take. If only there had been three of you instead, so that I could have had you in me, in every hole, simultaneously. If only I could be so replete with you now. If only....

Removing her cunt-scented hand from her crotch, she ripped open a second envelope. A single sheet of champagne-colored paper nested inside, folded in half around two more photographs. Circular and swooping, dark-green vowel-bubbles rolling across the lines, Marie-Sophie's letter was as short and curvy as the writer herself. The Polaroids wrenched Séverine's heart just as ruthlessly as her clit. Corinne. In ecstasy.

Séverine, my sister-love, forgive this bad little girl for not writing or calling as much as you would wish. Forgive me too for not yet having learned to use the computer, but it seems so cold. I am sometimes thoughtless but I am not heartless, so do not think that I do not love you just because I do not write.

I picked these because they reminded me of one reason I love you. You are beautiful because you are endless. You are beautiful because you satisfy but leave me wanting. You are beautiful because I can never get enough of the abandon that you achieve so effortlessly but that I myself cannot ever seem to enter. You see it, here, in the pictures I made of you.

Corinne bit your breasts, mauled them to make you sing with lust and agony, while Alain plunged into your cunt, spreading your legs wide, holding your ankles, slamming to the bottom of each stroke. He put your legs on his shoulders and reached for Cori's pussy. As he forced her open, she chewed your little breast so hard I thought you might bleed, so anguished she was with her own pleasure. Instead you came, shouting and arching, and then you came again as Corinne lunged for your other nipple and bit so sharply, sucking so hard, that I cringed. You screamed as they claimed you, the two of them, Alain's knuckles disappearing into Cori's impossibly wet cunt and completing the circuit, closed and complete. Your mouth was open in a scream of purest belonging. I envied you then, *ma soeur-amie,* but I could not help loving you as well.

Happy Birthday seems pale in comparison, but it is what your petite blondine who loves you wishes for you, sweet girl. Come back to us soon.

Séverine was grateful for the bits of explanation in the letters, for she could not clearly remember who had done what to her, or when, or in what order, the night before she flew away. She knew only that they had taken her, and did not stop. She had passed out briefly and had woken to find them still gently loving her, one mouth at each nipple, one mouth on her clitoris, three soft tongues calling her back to them. After they had roused her they had continued, for they were not yet satisfied. She was their whore that night, after all—a role she cherished, a task she was always dreadfully afraid she would not be able to fulfill to their satisfaction. It pleased her so deeply that they had continued even when she could not move, that they simply used her, forcing her to come, filling her, fucking her. It had felt right that Marie-Sophie and finally Corinne had fucked their sloppy-wet cunts against her mouth, that Alain's cock shot deep into her cunt and was then replaced with fingers, later a fist, and that then Alain was in her ass as well and still she remained the center, the fulcrum, the semen-soaked, arching and sobbing delirious fulcrum of the fuck.

Marie-Sophie's photographs were agonizing. Shot from the side, they showed Corinne's face contorted with enraged bliss, Alain's hand wedged into her from behind as he fucked hard into Séverine's juice-matted cunt. Séverine saw her own open mouth, throat taut with the force of her scream. Alain had been caught in mid-stroke, half of his long, lean cock pushing into her, Corinne's mouth digging hard, viciously, into her breast. In the second photo, Séverine could see the dark ring of tooth-marks, marks that had taken almost a month to fade. In her first lonely Canadian weeks Séverine had often brought herself to a homesick climax, eyes locked on the rings of toothprints where her sweet Corinne had marked and possessed her.

Corinne, Corinne, so matter-of-fact about the brutal part of love. From the start, she simply unleashed her need, seemed to know that my soul required it. Alain understands it perfectly, but he cannot hurt me like she can. He can use me as she cannot, though, with the one-eyed blindness of the male, that selfish possession that leaves me ragged. I marvel that Corinne requires that blindness and force as much as I. No wonder Sophie envied us the mathematics of our linked yielding, the commutative power of alchemical cock-violence opening Corinne's cunt, pushing her teeth into my flesh as I screamed with the obscene freedom of flight. As for Sophie, our gossamer girl with the liquid candlelight voice, I sense she goes there when she sings. She can only go there alone, but wants so much to go with some-one—anyone—else. We try, but fail, to take her there. She is one of us, but not one *with* us, and perhaps that is why we cannot do otherwise than love her as blindly, as unfailingly, as we do.

Tears in her eyes, Séverine skimmed her jeans down her thighs, swallowing back the longing that knotted her throat, trying to focus on the small, tight ball of shimmering heat that turned within her womb. She flipped her panties across the room with her foot as she tore open Corinne's envelope, aching with longing and lust. The photographs were face down against the letter. On the back of each photograph was a number, and she lay them in order, still face-down, on the bedspread beside her, as she knew Corinne wished her to do.

My sweet Séverine, angel whore, pretty pussy, greedy girl, how I miss you! It is your birthday, almost, and we have decided to remind you of us. I hope you remember how we like to use you, how much we love to make you ours, how much we like to fuck you while we tell you how we violate your pretty pussy, tender mouth, tight soft ass. Oh, how I miss making you writhe with vicious words and teeth and fingers, and oh, how the bed seems too wide without you to help fill it.

Take the first photograph, Séverine. Do you remember that instant? I asked Alain to take at least one picture of me filling your cunt with my fingers while I tortured those lovely little breasts of yours. I wanted to remind you of how it was when we began. It was just you and me then, you so skittish and afraid that you asked me to bind you tightly so that you could abandon yourself to the rapture. Do you recall how I tied you, wrists over your head, and slowly, gently worked you until you were able to let me touch you, not only your body but your heart? Can you remember how it felt to do this for the first time, bound, spread, fucked, used, nipples throbbing? Do you recall how you sobbed uncontrollably when you came, and I pushed you further, held you by nipples and cunt over the fires of your need like a spider being dangled over a candle flame by a thread of its own silk? I remember it well, and I remember your shuddering, sobbing as you begged me to ruin you.

This second photograph of you, I confess, I chose for beauty's sake. My pretty girls together open the innermost reserves of delight in my heart, for I can think of few things more lovely than your body moving with Marie-Sophie's. Look how she rides your face, your tongue and teeth, leaning forward, clawing your breasts, your hips bucking up out of sheer unconscious animal empathy with the nearness of her orgasm. That round little *crème-de-coeur* of a face gone savage with lust, the dark rose of your nipple just barely visible between two of her greedy fingers, the rolling swoops of her body hovering over the lean pantherine lines of yours! Such a spectacle, the two of you!

And then there is the simple fact that I love what you will take for me, what you will trust. Do you see in the third photo how you arched up for me as I pulled on the chain of the clamps, how you were almost like a marionette, pulled up by your cruelly pinched nipples, your motion forcing you further down on the dildo whose fat head I'd just worked into your ass? I had worked so much lube into you, but still I worried—you'd never taken anything so thick for me, not there. And so I held it in place, braced against my knee, just as you see me, one hand kneading your bubblegum clit, one hand pulling your back up off the quilts so that you had no choice but to slide down relentlessly onto the cock I'd chosen to violate you. I could feel your clit twitching under my fingers as you began to spasm, though the cock was only halfway inside you. I wish only that you could've seen how much it stretched you, for I know that it arouses you to know how I've forced you to open for me.

I made a puppet of you like that four times—four agonizing, beautiful times, until the cock was buried in you to its base. I can still hear your pleading: No no, it is too much! But oh, Séverine, in the next instant you begged me never to stop, to use you, to love you, to ruin you, to tear your sweet body, to fill you and never to let it end. I promised, and I meant it, and ten long slow times I pulled the cock almost out of your ass, and ten long thick wrenching times I plunged it hard back into you. Incoherent, you screamed and could not stop coming, and I yanked the clips from your nipples and sucked at your clit and rammed into you harder with the impossibly thick cock until you arched a final time and then lay limp, beyond yourself, unconscious, truly devastated by what you will accept only from my hands.

How I miss that, Séverine, my saucy brilliant love. I miss so much the way you let me touch you so deeply there, where you are desperate to be broken. In some ways it is in you, on and within your body, that I become the best and purest version of my self.

Bon anniversaire, ma petite. I miss you. I long to have you again, here, where you belong, at home. Soon. In the meantime, I hope that you will look at these photos, meager as they are, and remember that we miss you.

Séverine could not bear it. Her cunt and face dripped with different sorts of tears, and there were smears on the pages, on the glossy surfaces of the photos. Burying her face in the pillows, she rolled over onto her belly, hand sliding under her hip to her groin, left hand cupping her breast and pinching the nipple with a severity that made her gasp out loud. Feverish, heedless, she let present and past collide in a panorama of remembered sensation and the desperate need to be again what she saw in the Polaroids, to be her lovers' perfect whore. As she came, she sobbed out loud, though whether from the force of orgasm or the brutal longing she could not be sure.

In time Séverine lay quiet, fingers drenched and still tucked inside her. Softly from the other room she could hear the radio, CBC news muttering, like overhearing the neighbor's cocktail party through a half-open window. Wiping her hand on the duvet as she pushed herself up into a sitting position, she looked around her at the scattered pages, Polaroids lying around her like leaves. A wistful grin tweaked the corners of her mouth into curves as she gathered them, ordering the pages, stacking the photos into three piles face down on the edge of the bedside table. Then she saw a few lines on the back of Alain's first photograph, a note she had not noticed before.

> You are frozen like this in my mind. I am on the roof missing you, blowing smoke billows in which I search for your face. There is so much I miss. I love you.

She glowed deep inside as she reread his words, and the sharp edge of longing suddenly dulled and faded within her, the tightness of her chest easing as the gentle constancy of Alain's words penetrated her core. She missed all of them, yes, but suddenly it was not so unbearable somehow. She would take anything for them, even this, and it was with unashamed lust that she began to reread and review, fingers slipping between her legs, looking again at the photographs of her truest self, her love-bound self, caught in wondrous abjection, the constant and unflinching bearer of all the terrible weight of love.

ARROGANCE

Susan St. Aubin

SMALL, YOUNG FEMINIST, UNWILLING TO relinquish control. Not petite small; rather, unwilling to take up any significant space in the world. Holding herself in. Unwilling to demand anything from anyone; unwilling to let her emotions spill outside of her shell. Unwilling to yield to anyone, but unwilling to be powerful. To be strong and out of control. Consequently, unable to come. Me.

The second time I moved out of my parents' house, I lived with a beautiful, long-haired Goth-boy who owned more girly clothes than I did. Our bodies matched; everything he owned fit me. We couldn't decide how to feel about the movie *Lost Highway*. A woman stripping with a gun to her head shouldn't be sexy, we said. We weren't even convinced that consensual stripping *ought* to be sexy. Demeaning, we agreed. But hard cocks and wet cunts cannot lie. I tied my little Goth-boy to a chair and dressed myself in his clothing. I blared the movie's soundtrack and plugged in a strobe light. I taunted him as I shed to bare flesh and watched his ass squirm helplessly in his chair. Objectified? Degraded? I felt like a goddess.

Me. In thick black stockings that zipped up to my thigh. Swaying my black corduroy–clad hips in time to the music. Circling those hips. Thrusting those hips forward and back as black shirt buttons fell open one after another, revealing the only bra I owned, black and silky. My body blinked on and off in time to the strobe light behind him, making my movements seem at once drawn out and rapid-fire. I began to touch myself, running covered hands across my body and skin. White face, dark hair, white shoulders kissed by long black gloves, white stomach, black bra.

He said my face was cold as I circled him, my eyes daring him to want me as I took my zipper between thumb and forefinger and dragged my hand down my crotch. The black shorts fell to the floor, expanding the patch of white thigh glowing and disappearing as the tiny light ticked. I watched him with a faint smile, letting him take me in, his face tense, his lips parted. I stepped out of the shorts and tossed them scornfully into the corner. Black stockings, white legs, black cotton underwear with dark pubic hair spilling out the sides. Me, dancing, tormenting my bound lover, whose face betrayed rapture and ecstasy; this couldn't be wrong. I left him tied up as I straddled his body and swallowed him between my legs. My body flared as he gasped in pleasure.

It was the first time in weeks that I had been interested in sex. He was always wonderful and attentive and skilled; I just hadn't known what I wanted lately. I had been unable to figure it out on my own, and I did not want to frustrate him with the seemingly futile task. The things I sometimes thought I wanted, I felt guilty about. Not to touch, but to be touched. Not to crave, but to be craved. To be ravished, seduced, wanted. The longing felt selfish. Greedy. Insecure. And if I was seduced, ignited, pushed out of control by the will of another, I felt passive and powerless. Damned if I needed a man's sweet talk to turn me on. I certainly couldn't *ask* for it.

Taking it was another matter. He didn't need words when he was tied wide-eyed with the word "lust" screaming from every inch of his body. My stance commanded "Fall at my feet!" and I didn't have to ask for a thing.

During our last month together, my darkside lover saw the zippers on each of his beautiful dresses slide down my back. He saw my long hair burst from tight ponytails and cascade down my shoulders. He felt the steamy pulse of Lords of Acid, Nine Inch Nails, and Thrill Kill Kult as I looked him over, taunting. He touched my skin under strobe, candle, and computer light. Sometimes I'd untie him so that he could lick or fuck me; sometimes I caressed and stroked him in his chair. Sometimes, my dance was all, and afterward we slept, entangled and pressed close together. I was left soaring and intoxicated. I had never felt so high.

It was always I who stripped, always I who played the top and—I now recognized, despite the feminist propaganda—it was I who held the power as he beheld my naked body. This felt unfair. We shared the cooking and cleaning. We were gracious with sharing the car and the computer. Why should I monopolize the role of sex goddess? Why should only he be the one to grovel at my feet? Why weren't our desires more egalitarian? But when he tried stripping for me, he was self-conscious, and I grew bored. He looked beautiful, but his moves weren't sexy. We were not turned on. It didn't work. He wanted the chair; I wanted the spotlight. He untied me, and I stripped him naked and put him in handcuffs. We gorged on the sweetness of power and decadence, lighting us equally on fire. So deliciously self-indulgent. If I were a man, I'd want to be a drag queen.

I left Goth-boy and all his clothing behind when I went to college. I had to shop for my own sex-goddess image. I discovered credit cards and the Internet.

I had no lovers to entertain and render helpless, but still I wanted to be prepared. When my first package arrived, I asked my roommate what time she'd be home. Midnight, she said. It was eight o'clock. I cleared off my bed. The only mirror in the room was attached above my dresser, and standing on the bed was the only way I could see anything below my shoulders. The mirror was small and could only reflect me in portions, but it would have to do.

I started on top. I took the fishnet stockings I had worn as a Hot-Box girl in *Guys and Dolls,* cut holes in the feet for my hands and in the crotch for my head, and pulled them over my bra. I tried on every shirt I owned over that, but none of them looked right. I ditched the fishnets, put on the simple black button-down blouse I had acquired from Goth-boy, and turned on some music. I shifted back and forth in front of the mirror, balanced on my bed so that I could see my hips and torso, and tried unbuttoning the shirt to reveal my black bra. I rolled my shoulders back and ran my tongue across my lips, winking at myself in the mirror, and then giggled. I put my hands on my hips and slid them up my sides, caressing my naked stomach and dancing sensuously to the hot beat of the music. I loved how my body moved. Too much.

I had a borrowed white lacy nightgown that fell just to the thigh, and I decided to see how silly and wrong I'd look in girly white. But just for fun, I took my jeans off slowly. Adjusting my weight to frame my lower body in the pitiful mirror, I toyed with the fly buttons, moving my hips in provocative circles, bending to taunt the mirror with a cool gaze. I stepped out of the pants and kicked them aside but kept dancing, gliding my hands over my thighs, shifting to follow my hands in the mirror as they traveled up the edges of my stomach and squeezed my breasts.

I breathed heavily. I was getting wet.

Startled, I quickly put on the white lingerie and returned to the bed, now littered with clothing. I laughed at myself, feeling ridiculous, but still I swept everything to the floor and prepared to perform. Inspired by the torn fishnets beneath my feet, I jumped down and rummaged through the dresser, looking for a spare pair of black tights. I quit wondering what anyone else would want to see; this was no longer a seduction rehearsal for someone else. I was creating my dream girl. I tore clothes off hangers, dashing from the dresser to the closet, dimming the lights, dressing and re-dressing, and sorting through my tapes and CDs. Finally, I was ready.

Shoulders thrown back, chin lifted, covered neck to ankles in a black cloak, I stood on my bed. I reached with my toe for the CD player and stepped on "play," filling the room with a dark low beat. My stomach fluttered. For several measures I just stared, standing still with my icy gaze. Then slowly I opened one edge of the cloak to reveal a thin center line of my body in white lace and black leggings, and then let the cloak drop again. I felt a wave of excitement but kept my face cold and still. I teased my eyes this way twice more and then pushed the cloak off my shoulders, spreading my arms as it crumpled at my feet. One corner of my mouth curled up in a wicked smile, and once again I began to move.

I danced one number just like that—white lace over black tights, running my fingers over the silky fabric, exploring the curves underneath, turning and gyrating to show off my hot clothing from every angle, feeling my ass, moving to keep that mirror just where I wanted it.

My gaze was riveted on my body. I didn't pretend there was someone else watching me. The girl in the mirror was mine. She was doing this for me. This body, this sexy body, was mine. *I live inside this body.* My back arched and my head turned, sinking my teeth into my shoulder as my fingers clawed her thighs, breasts, and stomach. I wanted her. I wanted to touch her, to feel her, to lick her.... What am I *doing,* I asked myself, that's *me* I'm drooling over; my body I'm touching...*worshiping...* *God!* Fucking arrogant bitch!

But a wet cunt cannot lie.

I watched the girl in the mirror. Her hips churned, and she teased the tops of her thighs with the tip of her short lacy lingerie. With her fist she gathered fabric slowly at the waist, raising the hemline slightly, and I could hear my heavy breath as her covered pussy came into sight, knowing there was nothing between the tights and her naked cunt. To torture me, she dropped her hands, and the dress fell halfway to her knee. She smiled and reached for the scissors.

Balancing one leg on the bedpost, she brought the edge of the short white gown to her waist and scraped the tip of the scissors along her leg from ankle to thigh. She heard my anguished moan. Without hesitating, she sliced an opening in the tights across the front of her upper thigh while I gaped in fascination. She snipped a hole in the other leg, and then dropped the scissors and resumed dancing. Her hands slid under the black nylon, and her whole body was lost in erotic ecstasy as she widened the gap with her fingers. She kneeled to pick up the scissors again, still holding the dress up at the waist, her devilish eyes sparkling. She circled a hand behind her left thigh and palmed her ass, her nails leaving a red trail across her skin as her taut fingers tore through the fabric. Next she attacked from the right and released both legs of the tights from the crotch section. She grasped this top piece and in one violent motion ripped it from her body. The dress dropped and covered her coarse black fur the moment she was exposed, and a whimper tickled my throat. I could hear her panting.

She rolled her tights down her thigh until they teased the lace edge of her silky dress. Her body swayed. She took the dress by the shoulders and pulled it over her head, still moving in a lewd trance. I could see every curve of her smooth body as she bent and lowered herself, surveying her form. Her white flesh shone, bare except for the bra and the black tights stretching up to the base of her thigh. She swept her hair up in two clenched fists, and then let it fall. As she lifted a leg to slowly roll the tights off the ends of her toes, she looked up and eyed me with a haughty gaze. I had to fuck her.

I ripped off my bra and collapsed to the sheets, reaching one hand up to clasp the bedpost as the other dove for my clit. As my arm lifted, the smell of salt and sweat hit me, a luscious slap across the face. *What am I doing?* my brain screamed, as I inhaled again and felt my back arch in desire. My scent surrounded me, intoxicated me; my other hand floated toward my face. I closed my eyes as I breathed in the sweet sex smell from my fingertips. I resisted the gluttonous urge to taste them and reached instead for my vibrator. My body shuddered as I moved the cheap plastic egg between my thighs, and the only thing keeping my sounds down to heavy breathing was my fear of the dorm's thin walls.

*God, my roommate could come home at any minute...*but my fear was quickly forgotten. Something was happening to me. My body was doing things it had never done before. I pressed the slimy egg against my cunt, and my cunt pressed back. My body was convulsing. The egg moved under my hands in rhythm to my body's contractions, and I gasped in wonder. Never mind the pleasure; *what strange thing was this majestic body doing?* This *woman* body, this unexplored... God. Tiny moans escaped my lips. The contractions stopped.

What just happened to me? I lay, stunned, across my black sheets, staring at the ceiling but seeing only stars. Where was I? Who was I? Was I, me, really this majestic woman-goddess? I ran my hands up and down my soft, naked skin and closed my eyes in wonder. This was heaven. Did I love the caresses, or did I love to caress? Or both? Or was I just in love with sex and my body and the universe? I lifted a lazy arm to turn out the light and rested, drifting off slowly amid my dissipating smells and calming heartbeat.

It's been a year since that night. I just bought myself a sexy, silk black dress. It cost less than the vibrator that's as big as my arm and puts to shame the cheap egg that first taught my body how to scream. I have no lover to strip for; I haven't stripped for another human since the days of Goth-boy. I bought the dress just for me. Me, my magic wand, and the girl in the full-length mirror, larger than life.

BETWEEN THE TOES

Tara Alton

RAIN STREAMED ACROSS THE SKYLIGHT OF MY loft, reminding me of the rivers of sweat that used to create patterns down my lover's back. I was enticed by that image, the contrast between the dry skin and the wet. I've always loved what lies between two things, especially between two people entwined in the night.

I sat on my bed, wearing nothing but a tank top and a thong. I was waiting for him to come home, but it was past midnight. The gym was closed. He should be here, but he wasn't. As on so many recent nights, he was out with his martial-arts friends, talking about his upcoming matches. With my friends, I had been talking a lot about my loneliness.

But it was too late to call anyone now. Besides, I was beginning to sound like a broken record, lamenting my lack of sex and male companionship. My girlfriend, Michelle, told me maybe I should do something about it. Like what? Like call a chat line, she suggested.

I flipped through a local alternative newspaper, to the advertisements for singles chat lines. They were free for women. Michelle had told me she'd blotted out hours of silence late at night talking to strangers. I found an advertisement. Over 3,000 callers every day! True, I was shy and I didn't like bars. But did I have the nerve to call?

Gazing at the alluring man in the picture talking to a pretty woman on the phone made me wonder what it would be like to talk to someone I didn't know. I tried to imagine it. I closed my eyes and slid my hand beneath my thong. I dialed the number.

After a few awkward conversations, I spoke to a man with a smooth and sexy voice, the type of voice I could imagine offering to buy me a margarita on a sun-soaked beach, and then whisking me away for a night of dancing. I learned he was a high-powered stockbroker who was stressed out by his job. He wanted to find a woman he could spoil and pleasure. It was his desire to make a woman happy. And he was glad to hear I wasn't a stripper on the line trying to drum up business.

I didn't tell him that I had a physically powerful boyfriend who had been ignoring me, nor did I tell him I was so naive that I didn't even know about these phone lines until a girlfriend told me. What I did tell him was what I enjoyed: Rainy evenings. Chocolate mousse before dinner at an expensive restaurant. Two people so tuned in that the mere thought of the other made them tremble.

He asked if I had ever entertained the idea of having my feet worshipped. I hadn't. He called me a "goddess." I felt an excited chill. No one had ever called me that before.

I paused, nervous from the sense of power evoked by the word. Once, I had held my lover's hands over his head while I made love to him on top. I had really gotten off, making him call me "beautiful one."

"Please don't call me that," I said to the man on the phone.

"All right," he whispered. "But will you let me buy you a pair of five-inch red leather shoes and leave them at the store for you? As a thank-you for talking to me."

"Why?" I asked.

"Because you've been so straightforward with me."

I didn't know what to say.

"Please accept them," he said.

"I can't," I said. "I don't know you."

"Imagine your beautiful feet in a pair of wonderfully sexy shoes," he said. "It would make me happy to do this."

By the time I hung up the phone, I had accepted them; after all, he'd sounded so forlorn when I'd refused.

The next day on the way to the shoe store it occurred to me that he might be watching. He could be looking me over; I had no idea what he looked like. Would he approve of me? I'd worn my usual white T-shirt, jeans, and tennis shoes.

I looked around the mall. Was he here? The shop he'd selected was no ordinary place. They had PVC court shoes, platforms, and thigh-high leather boots.

The gift was waiting for me—a pair of five-inch patent leather ankle-strap sandals. Bright red. I thought maybe they had made a mistake in the size, but the clerk assured me that with a five-inch heel, I'd need the larger size for comfort.

That night, I called the chat line. His message beeped in. I wanted to ask him if he had been at the mall, but I didn't—just thanked him for the beautiful shoes. By the time I hung up the phone, I had agreed to meet him. He said he wanted to indulge me, to worship my feet at a swinger's club. I'd heard of the place— a health club during the day that at night catered to "adult" themes.

Looking down at my toes, I wondered if I was doing the right thing. I liked my lover. I cared about him and I was attracted to him—but I didn't feel like a priority in his life anymore. We used to spend so much time together, but now if I saw him once a week I was lucky. I couldn't even remember the last time we'd gone out to dinner.

I didn't think Michelle had ever met anyone from the chat lines. But I was so lonely, I needed to do something. Would my lover break up with me if he found out? Would he even care? Would he freak? I had no idea.

That afternoon, I lavished attention on my feet. I gave myself a pedicure and painted my toenails red to match the shoes. I wore them that night with a red slip dress cut so low you could see the sprinkle of freckles trickling down into my cleavage.

Underneath, I wore only a thong and a pair of thigh-high stockings. I hadn't worn such a "come and get me" outfit in ages. I felt like a statuesque Amazon towering in my new shoes: The mirror reflected my long, sleek calves.

As I left the building, I imagined my lover coming up the sidewalk and seeing me like this. What would I say? He hadn't seen me dressed like this in a long time. I hurried to my car.

It had been my idea to meet my stranger at a riverside bar near the club for a drink first. That way our initial meeting would be at a public place, and I could gracefully exit if need be. As I walked into the bar, I felt a flutter in my stomach that I hadn't felt since my swimming meets in high school.

He was in his late forties, slightly graying at the temples, and he smelled like musk. He was nothing like my lover, who ran around in sweats all the time and ate huge amounts of steamed vegetables to bulk up. This man certainly didn't have his muscular stomach, but he had an attentive charm.

There was such a pleased expression on his face when he saw me wearing the shoes that I blushed. He couldn't take his eyes off me.

When we got to the club, we separated to change. In the women's locker room I took off my outfit and wiggled into the complimentary toga. I slid a silver toe ring I'd bought at an art fair onto one of my toes.

I was nervous, but he gently guided me by the small of my back and showed me the pool, saunas, and whirlpools. I flushed when we got to the room with the adult movies. If you sat on the floor, you were open to anyone who approached you, but if you sat on the sofas, you were saying you weren't interested—yet. One curvaceous woman was attended by two men while another woman looked on.

He led me to a quiet spot where several couples were engaged in private conversation, sat me down on a chair, and settled at my feet. I felt awkward at first, but then he began to massage my feet. His hands worked the bones with a rolling motion. He paid individual attention to each toe. He stretched every joint. He didn't tickle.

Just when I thought I would melt, he raised my pinky toe to his mouth and sucked on it. My pussy clenched as he nibbled on my skin. He turned his attention to the toe with the ring on it. Gently, he pulled the toe into his mouth, and when it emerged, the ring was gone. He took my other foot, extended a toe, and slid it into his mouth. With his tongue and teeth, he slid the ring back on to it.

I gripped the chair. My legs were weak. No one had ever gotten me this turned on.

"My God," I said.

I'd never had my toes inside someone's mouth before. The feeling was intense, as was the look in his eyes. He worked his tongue between my toes, touching tender skin I'd never even known existed. I squirmed with heat. Seeing my reaction, he used his tongue to prod and poke.

A couple of the women around us were watching. He lowered my foot to the floor and rested his head on my knee. I stroked his hair. I noticed that a lovely redhead's feet had caught his attention. She had tiny feet with a spray of freckles on her pale skin. He looked up at me expectantly, and I realized he was asking me for permission.

"Go ahead," I said.

Like an obedient pet, he crawled over on his hands and knees and worshiped her feet. Next he found a brunette with high arches and a ticklish spot, and then an Asian woman with a delicate lily tattoo near her ankle.

After the last lick of her toes, he looked as if he were satisfied—but I wasn't. He had nibbled heels, sniffed insteps, and massaged toes with his big, manly hands. I didn't know what was more exciting, the thought of his licking my toes again or of watching his mouth on another woman's feet—but I wanted something more intimate.

"Let's go," I said.

We showered, changed, and met in the lobby. I thought maybe we could go for another drink and get to know each other better, but the cool water of the shower hadn't calmed the throbbing in my pussy. The moment I saw him, the urge to put my feet in his lovely mouth again got the best of me.

One of the lobby rooms was empty. I pulled him inside.

"Get down on your knees," I ordered.

He immediately obeyed. I started to take off my shoes, but he stopped me, lay down on the floor, and brought my heel over his mouth.

"Tell me to let you fuck my mouth with your heel," he said.

I hesitated. "It's a sharp heel," I said. "I don't want to hurt you."

"I'll show you."

Gently lifting my foot, he guided my shoe up and down, sliding my heel in and out between his lips. It scraped across his tongue.

"Let me fuck your mouth," I said.

He opened his mouth a little, and I ran the edge of it across his top teeth. I could see inside his mouth. It was a new and weird experience, penetrating a man, but it was getting me wetter by the minute. I could see him looking up my skirt as his lips sucked my heel. I inched up the fabric.

Sliding off my shoe, he ripped open my silk thigh-highs and exposed my foot. All my toes slid into his mouth. He sucked them in, pulling my foot in and out. It was too much: I really was fucking his mouth with my foot. I pulled my skirt up to my hips, pushed down my thong, and fingered my clit. His eyes were riveted on mine.

I pulled my foot out of his mouth and flexed my toes. His tongue slid between them, wet, whirling, finding the tender spot that sent me over the edge.

I came like a wild woman, my voice resonating through the silence of the lobby, my arms and legs going numb, my ears buzzing.

Looking down at him, his eyes glazed, his chest heaving, I wondered what else he could do to me. Between my toes. Between my arms. Between my thighs.

When we left, he asked if he could buy me another pair of shoes next weekend, and if he could have the privilege of going with me to select them. Then he would take me to a theme hotel.

I felt as if I'd been transformed from a submissive couch potato waiting for a lover into an adventurous goddess. And, I must admit, my feet were itching to try on shoes.

I told him yes.

STRANGE BEDFELLOWS

Randi Kreger

"MY MOST POWERFUL SEXUAL FANTASY IS about making love to my sister," Robert said quietly, right in her ear.

"Excuse me?" she said, freezing, the champagne glass halfway to her lips.

He moved closer, his breath hot against her neck.

"A few days ago you asked me what my most intense sexual fantasy is. I said it was being with two women at once, but I lied. My hottest fantasy is about my sister."

He looked at her face for some kind of reaction. Nothing. She rested her glass on the edge of the balcony railing and looked out at the long driveway leading to the estate.

It's finally done, he thought. Whatever happens, happens.

"Let me see if I have this straight," she said after a moment. Her voice was low and intense.

"The other day we're lying in bed, naked, getting ready to fuck. I ask you what you think about when you jerk off. You tell me some lie about having one women sit on your cock while the other straddles your face. Now, here we are at this major fund-raiser for your boss. You're wearing your best suit, I'm in a black velvet cocktail dress, hair done up, gold earrings—there are a hundred people all around us, your professional future is at stake—and you've chosen this moment to tell me you want to make love to your *sister?*" The word "sister" came out like a hiss.

Rob took a nervous sip from his gin and tonic and glanced around to see if anyone was listening. Susan always got a little loud after a few drinks. Luckily, the crowd had drifted from the third floor balcony toward the spacious living room, where Hal was scheduled to give an informal speech.

"Not exactly," he said, swirling his glass and watching the ice bob up and down. "Sometimes I do think about two women. I just think about having sex with my sister a lot more often." He looked up to see if she was smiling. She wasn't. She was staring at him in disbelief. He gulped the rest of his drink, wishing there were more, and then continued. "Susan, for months I've been trying to get up the courage to tell you what happened between my sister and me when we were kids. It just hit me that if I didn't say something right now, I might never find the nerve. And you deserve to know about it before we get married."

"Something *happened* between the two of you?" she asked. "You mean...this isn't just a fantasy?"

"Well," he said hesitantly, "Yes, something did happen. The summer I turned 14. We were alone in the house..."

"Wait!" she interrupted, grabbing her beaded purse from a nearby table. "I don't want to talk about this. I need some time. I...I need to be alone right now." She darted into the mansion, spilling some of her drink, nearly tripping on her new high-heeled pumps, not bothering to acknowledge the gray-haired lady she passed on her way inside.

He groaned when he saw the woman approaching. *Please, not Vera. Not now.*

"There you are!" said Vera as she waddled out onto the balcony, both chins bobbing up and down. "Congratulations on your engagement! Susan looks so lovely tonight."

He forced a smile. "She is beautiful, Vera, thank you. And thank you for staffing the welcome table, too. A lot of important people are going to be here tonight."

"That's what I came to talk to you about," she huffed, waving a piece of paper in front of his face. "Look how they misspelled Mr. Peck's name tag!" He glanced at the label.

MR. JOHN BECK, PRESIDENT, NATIONAL RIGHT TO LIFE

It was one of those days.

"Good catch, Vera," he said. "You know how much money Right to Life donated to Hal's campaign. Why don't you see if you can find Mr. Wirthington—Peter should know where he is—and ask if he has any correction fluid you can use to white out the bottom of the 'B' to make a 'P.'"

"Wonderful idea," she said, and wandered off. When Vera was gone he crumpled into a wooden folding chair and rested his head in his hands. He sat there agonizing for several minutes. Why hadn't he trusted his instincts and kept quiet? Where had Susan gone? What was going through her mind right now? And what could he do or say to repair the damage?

He had thought she could handle the truth. After all, they were so open with each other about sex: They used exotic sex toys, tried different positions, and watched porn movies naked in the middle of the day with the shades pulled down.

Susan loved to role-play during sex. Despite his pain, he smiled at the memory of the time she had played the professor and he the eager student willing to trade sex for a good grade.

A month ago they had pretended she was auditioning for the cheerleading squad and he was the judge. Dressed in nothing but an old pleated skirt and knit top from high school, she stood on the kitchen table, twirling a baton. He remembered the way her skirt had whirled up, revealing creamy white thighs and her smooth, hairless pussy. God, how they had fucked that night, again and again.

So he had decided to tell her the truth. Now she would never look at him the same way again. Maybe she would never look at him again, period.

"Shit!" he yelled, enraged at the injustice of his situation. He slammed his fist against the wood railing.

"Now, I don't think that Troy and Angela would appreciate you defacing their property." Startled, he looked up to see Peter, Hal's campaign manager, standing in the doorway. Great. Now he'd lose any chance at the press secretary job, too. "Hey kid, it's just a fucking name tag," said Peter, lighting a cigarette. "So what are you doing here, anyway? You should be downstairs in case any media types show up."

Rob mumbled something in response and tried to go inside. But Peter grabbed him by the arm. "Hey, did you see that John Potter is here, schmoozing it up?" Peter chuckled. "It's strange to see him here after he and Hal sparred so publicly on that stadium tax plan. But I guess politics does make strange bedfellows." He ground his cigarette into the balcony floor.

"Yeah, Pete, I guess it does." Rob went inside and made his way through the ornate hallways of the mansion to the grand staircase. He stopped at a spacious landing halfway down the stairs and scanned the crowd of well-dressed partygoers, looking for Susan.

"Which sister was it, Laura or Stephanie?"

He spun around. Susan was right behind him on the landing, her bright red lipstick freshly applied. She was wavering slightly; was it from the champagne or his declaration?

"Laura," he said. "Of course it was Laura. When I was 14, Stephanie was only 11!"

She looked relieved. "Thank God," she said, proceeding on down the stairs. He grabbed her shoulders, turned her around, and looked into her eyes from the step above. "Susan," he said, holding her shoulders tightly. "Did I screw everything up? Please tell me this doesn't make any difference and that you're still going to marry me."

She looked down for a moment, avoiding his eyes. "Of course I'm going to marry you. It's all right. It's just a surprise." She stopped and looked up at him, her brown eyes flashing. "I've seen the two of you together a couple of times, and I had no idea. I guess I just don't understand."

"Laura won't talk about it. She just laughs and says we did some crazy things when we were kids."

"Then—are you still attracted to her?" she asked, looking directly into his eyes. "Are you saying that you fantasize about her *now,* or that you did when you were a teenager?"

He paused. He couldn't risk telling her the truth. "It's in the past."

She took his hands. "Tell me what happened, then. I need to know."

"You want me to tell you right now? Here?" he asked, feeling guilty and confused. Twenty minutes ago she'd said she didn't want to talk about it.

"Right here, right now," she said. "Besides, no one can hear us."

He looked around. She was right. They were alone on the stairs. She stood with her back to the crowd, and he could talk to her, watch for media people, and appear to listen to the speech at the same time. He didn't really need to hear the speech—after all, he had written it.

"All right, I'll tell you." He lowered his voice and paused for a moment. "I was 14 and she was 16, and our parents were at work all day. Stephanie was at camp, I think. One day Laura and I were having an argument and I was angry, so I mooned her. She just laughed like it was a big joke."

Susan nodded. Encouraged, he continued.

"And, well, mooning her turned me on. So I did it a couple more times that week, leaving my pants down a little longer each time. Once or twice, as a joke, she came up behind me and pulled my pants down in back. Then she started to moon me back, too."

"I bet seeing her ass got you very hard." Susan said. It was a statement, not a question.

Maybe she didn't understand, but she knew him well. "Yeah. Sometimes I was so turned on after seeing her I would go into the bathroom to jerk off. The whole time, I'd be fantasizing about showing her my cock." He looked down at Susan on the step below him, his eyes drifting from her face to her breasts. They were very conspicuous in her low-cut dress. He rubbed her palms with his thumbs, gentle little circles.

"Finally I was so turned on I just had to flash her. I pulled down my pants in front of her—just for an instant—and showed her my hard dick. She was shocked at first, but then she laughed. So the next day I did it again, but I kept my pants down for a lot longer."

Suddenly Peter's voice interrupted them from the foyer below. "Thank you all so much for coming here this evening, and a special thanks to Troy and Angela Wirthington, our hosts for this evening," he said. "You know, a few years ago our party did a lot of talking about 'family values.' But then in the rush to appease moderates, we seemed to forget where we stood on vital issues. School prayer. Abortion. School choice. The death penalty. But one man didn't forget his principles. He didn't forget—and he didn't let anyone else forget either. May I introduce Hal Schmidt, our next state senator!"

They joined in the applause from the stairway. But before it died down, he grabbed Susan's hand more firmly and guided her to the top of the landing. It was quieter and more private there, but he could still hear what was going on. She was taking this better than he had dared hope.

"All right. So you were showing Laura your erect penis," she prompted. "Then what happened?"

They were standing in a dark corner in the second floor hallway, Susan's back to the wall. He looked around. They were alone.

He paused, recalling the chain of events. "A few days later, something happened that really changed things. I was lying on the floor in my pajama bottoms and watching TV. I didn't even realize Laura was in the room. Suddenly she was in front of me, in her PJs too, blocking the TV and tugging like hell on the hems of my pajama bottoms, near the feet. She pulls them off and starts running away with them, and I follow her, naked now, and she goes to our parents' room and I catch her and grab *her* pajama bottoms and pull them off. She's rolling around the king-sized bed, laughing, her hair flying all over the place, and I'm stronger than she is, so I rip off her top too. Buttons are flying all over the place, and we start wrestling on the bed trying to pin each other down. And we're nude. And I'm as hard as hell."

The image came rushing to him again: Laura pinned down on the bed. She is laughing, her head rolling from side to side, her shoulder-length blonde hair in her face as she half-heartedly struggles to get away. He looks down at her full breasts, which are jiggling up and down, her nipples pink and erect. His cock is brushing against her stomach, and he could see from the excitement in her eyes that she is as turned on as he is.

"Then what happened? Did you stay on the bed?" Susan said, interrupting his reverie. He looked up and realized he was leaning against the wall, Susan almost pressed up against him. The memory of his nude sister, an image he must have invoked for hundreds of masturbation sessions, was having its usual effect on his cock. Applause and laughter drifted up the stairs.

"No, we got up and tried to find all the buttons," he said. "But we had definitely crossed some kind of line. We hung around together for the next few hours, naked. The next day I got out of bed, without any clothes on, and I went into her room to wake her up. She was already out of bed, walking around nude. From that day on we just hung out together naked, eating cereal, doing laundry or doing whatever, until she had to go to work in the afternoon."

"You were erect?" she asked, bending down to pick an imaginary piece of lint off his knee.

"Practically the whole time," he answered, watching her closely. She had to know that in that position her breasts were totally visible. He watched them sway back and forth in her strapless push-up bra and resisted the urge to cup them in his hand. After flicking off the lint, Susan began playing with the buttons of his shirt and grazing her fingers across his chest. Was this the same Susan who had run away from him on the balcony? He didn't understand what was going on, but he wasn't going to ruin it by asking questions.

"It's hard to explain, but we played things out on two levels," he said, praying that no one would come up the stairs. "On one level it was innocent, teasing, fun stuff. Either of us could have backed out at any time, saying it was just a joke. But on another level it was obviously very sexual."

"Did you ever see Laura's pussy? Not just her pubic hair, but her slit?" Susan asked, running a finger along the top of his belt. His stomach and balls were tight and his cock was rock-hard now, pressing uncomfortably against his briefs. He glanced around and adjusted himself. Susan seemed to pretend not to notice.

"Yes, several times," he said huskily. He had to put a stop to this. Someone could come up at any minute. He strained to hear the speech so that he could judge how much more time alone they had. But all he could make out were a couple of phrases: "tax and spend" and "welfare reform." Now, where had he put the anti-Democrat section?

"The first time I really saw her pussy, we were watching TV. Laura was lying on her back with her knees up and I was by her feet, kind of at a right angle. She couldn't see exactly where I was looking, but I think she knew she was giving me a show."

"What did you think of the way it looked?" Susan asked, her fingers moving down his pants leg, inches from his swollen cock. He reached out and touched the bare tops of her breasts.

"It looked like the prettiest flower you ever saw—just like yours," he said, running his fingers over her nipples and feeling them harden. Through his pants she began running her thumb and two fingers up and down the length of his rigid cock. He moaned softly.

"I bet you couldn't wait until she went to work so you could jerk off," she whispered, nibbling on his earlobe and rubbing the back of his neck with her other hand.

"I could never wait that long—my balls hurt too much," he said, his cock throbbing. "I'd jerk off in the bathroom while she was dressing for work. She knew exactly what I was doing because I'd be soft afterward, and she'd tease me, saying, 'Ooooh, and what were *you* doing, little brother?' One day she said, 'You don't have to go to the bathroom to do that, you know. We're open about a lot of things. You can do that here.'"

Susan's eyes widened. He knew that "fuck me now" look on her face. Glancing down, he saw a small wet spot forming on his pants. He needed it too, badly. They had to get out of there. He didn't give a shit about Peter, and he sure couldn't go back downstairs.

Suddenly, Susan took his hand. "Follow me," she ordered, leading him to a closed door off the hallway. "I saw this room earlier; it's perfect." She led him in and closed the door.

They seemed to be in a small guest bedroom. It was decorated with rattan baskets, hand-woven rugs, and colorful pottery that Angela must have picked up on one of her jaunts to South America. The walk-in closet was open, and woolen winter clothes were piled high on the double bed. The room smelled slightly of mothballs and dried flowers.

Susan led him to the far side of the bed away from the door. "No one will see us here," she said, kneeling on the floor and slipping down the straps of her dress. God, what a wife he had chosen.

"Tell me," she said, taking off her bra, revealing her firm breasts and erect nipples. He leaned over and sucked on one of them, but she pushed his mouth away. "No, tell me what happened next."

He caressed her with his hands. "One day we sat on the opposite ends of the couch and I started stroking my cock, using my pre-cum for lube as I watched Laura rub her pussy." He pulled up Susan's dress and fondled the crotch of her panties. They were soaked. "I only lasted a minute before I came all over my chest and stomach." He put his fingers to his nose to smell Susan's fragrance.

"Yes. Yes. Touch me," she moaned, pulling her panties down over her legs. He noticed that her pantyhose weren't the regular kind; they only went up to her thigh. He slid his fingers between Susan's slick pussy lips and tried to unbutton his pants with the other hand. She reached out to help him. "Did Laura touch you? Did you touch her?"

"Not that time. But a couple of weeks later I finally got her to jerk me off while she let me touch her tits. I couldn't believe how good her hand felt on my cock. So much better than my own." He needed to be inside her. "Susan. Get on top of me," he said, pulling his pants and briefs down to his knees, freeing his cock at last.

"Call me 'Laura,'" she said, quickly removing her panties and lifting up her dress. She straddled him. "Fuck me, little brother. Fuck me." She lowered herself over his cock, rubbing the swollen head against her wet lips, and finally slipping him inside.

As she moved on top of him, he struggled to hold himself back. "Laura," he whispered, closing his eyes and visualizing his older sister's face, her glistening pussy lips, the way her hand had felt on his cock. "It feels so good to fuck you at last."

Laura was thrusting fast now, squeezing him, the warmth and wetness of her cunt enveloping him, forcing everything out of his mind but a primitive need to fuck, to come, to pump his seed into his sister. "Laura, Laura," he moaned.

"Steve. Yes. Fuck. Me." She groaned. She was coming now, crying out, and he finally let himself spurt into her, grunting, feeling the sharp pain of her nails digging into her shoulder.

Suddenly there was a loud knock on the door. They froze. "Hello? Is anyone in there?" A drunken giggle. Then a different voice. "That's not the bathroom, silly. They said the end of the hall to the left." The knocking stopped. Then a faint voice said, "Well, I tell you, I heard *something*."

Silence. Susan lay quietly against him, breathing heavily, her arms around his shoulders, her face buried in his neck. His softening cock was still in her, bathed in her juices and his own cum.

But he felt uneasy, as though there was something he had forgotten, something he should remember. They lay there a moment. Then it came to him.

"Susan," he murmured softly, looking up at the ceiling and running his fingernails lightly up and down her back. "Why did you just call me by your brother's name?"

CAL'S PARTY

Lisa Prosimo

FOUNDATION. EYELINER. MASCARA.

I didn't want to go to the party.

Blush. Lipstick.

The towel I was wearing fell to the floor. I bent to pick it up, and my right temple throbbed.

"Shit."

"You almost ready, Abby? It's getting late."

Steve stood in the doorway. His eyes swept across my naked body. He smiled. "Wear that black dress. The one that stretches and stops here." He tapped his leg, midthigh. "And your 'fuck me' shoes. The ones with the strap at the ankle."

"Steve...I have a headache. I really don't feel like—"

He walked into the room, stood behind me, and wrapped his arms across my waist. His breath tickled my ear. "Hey, no problem," he whispered. "I've got just the right medicine for that. One hit and your headache's gone." He stuck his tongue in my ear and licked lightly.

I pulled away and turned to face him. His face was flushed, his eyes bright. "I don't want any 'medicine,' Steve. Though I see you've taken some."

"One line. A skinny, tiny little line. Cal gave me some."

"What a pal."

Steve walked to the closet and pulled the black dress off its hanger. He brought it to me. "Come on, Abby. I don't want to make the grand entrance." I took the dress, slipped it over my head, and pulled it down. The fabric settled over the contours of my body. "Oh, yeah. Fabulous."

I couldn't wait to swallow a Motrin.

The house was crowded, as usual. As usual, the music was too loud, the lights too bright, the food table too perfect. Plump, pink shrimp covered two large cones in a flawless symmetrical pattern, flowers of puff pastry adorned the face of each round of Brie. Waiters in tight black T-shirts and snug white shorts carried trays of champagne. Tonight's theme: muscled blonds with chiseled features, none under six feet tall. Each wore a small diamond on his left earlobe—a gift from the host, no doubt. Cal was always generous with his waiters.

"Abby! Steve!" Cal moved toward us, his arms flung wide, his heavy rump bouncing with each step. He was blond, too. Last time I'd seen him, he had red hair. He'd called it his "Irish Queen" look. The stud in his left ear was bigger than the waiters'. "Oh, my God, don't you look gorgeous, Abby! It's been ages. I've really missed you, girl! Kiss, kiss."

"Kiss, kiss back at you," I said.

Cal turned and enveloped Steve in a crushing bear hug. "And you, you gorgeous thing." He let go of Steve and pulled a handkerchief from his breast pocket, mopped his brow, and caught the drip from his nose. He sniffed. "So, how are you two love-birds?"

"We're great," Steve said. "Wonderful, in fact." He smiled at me. I smiled back.

"Good, good. Well...enjoy!" He bounced away, his arms outstretched to the newest arrivals.

"I'm starved," Steve said. "Let's get something to eat."

"I'm not all that hungry."

Steve shrugged. "OK. I'll get something, and you can mingle."

One of the blond boys carrying a full tray stopped in front of me. I took two flutes of champagne from him and walked into the great room. In one corner, a quartet banged out an A.M. hit. My temple banged along. I settled onto one of the over-stuffed sofas and downed the first glass of champagne, and then sipped the second. People I'd met before nodded and smiled, but there were a lot of people I'd never seen. Still, it was Cal's typical crowd, made up of stylish men and women, all possessing a type of eclectic beauty. These parties always gave me the feeling that I was trapped on some opulent soundstage with a bunch of extras from Central Casting. Five years ago, when I'd first met Cal, I found that aspect attractive. I was a girl from Idaho who had come to Hollywood, sure my talents and good looks would land me a plum role in a blockbuster movie. After all, in Boise I had been a star. I even had a college degree. Who could resist?

Lots of people resisted.

A waiter offered me another glass of champagne. I took it. "Abby."

I looked up. Lloyd Thomas smiled down at me.

"It's been a long time, Abby. You look wonderful."

Lloyd looked wonderful, too, but I didn't say so. He sat down, took my hand, turned it over, and kissed my palm.

"How's...Steve, is it?"

"Yes. Fine, thank you."

"He's the fellow who builds things, right?"

"Yes. He and his brother have a construction company. And you?"

He smiled. "Still selling junk bonds."

"Ah…I see. Better be careful."

"I'm always careful, Abby." He smiled.

A tall blonde walked over. "Lloyd? Did you want to get something to eat?" she asked.

Lloyd introduced us. Her name was Jenny. Jenny was happy to make my acquaintance, she said. After a few moments of meaningless chatter, Lloyd and Jenny headed for the food table in the other room.

Lloyd Thomas had been my first man, so to speak. He took me to my premier party at Cal's. I met him while working as a temp at his brokerage firm. At first, Cal's parties were fun. Sometimes they lasted a weekend, sometimes longer. One room at the back of an old house in Boyle Heights wasn't exactly my idea of home, so I often stayed at Cal's, breaking several dozen eggs to feed Cal and his boys breakfast. While I cooked, I answered an endless stream of calls that came in from his friends and various boy lovers. I could stay as long as I wanted if I promised not to get in his way, and I made sure I didn't. Why wouldn't I want to stay? There was always plenty of food and drink, plus an abundant supply of nose candy. I remember once, in a mild rush of drugs, roving hands, and tongues, being struck by the notion that I had to be one of the luckiest girls alive. That enlightenment came at the same moment I did.

The throbbing in my temple increased, helped along by the champagne. I walked out to the patio and sat in one of the chairs and watched several men and women play in the hot tub. One of the men was sitting outside the tub, his feet in the water. A head belonging to a brunette bobbed up and down between his legs. She held his penis inside her lips and slid them down over his shaft slowly, until it disappeared. She did it without the use of her hands, and I had to admire her expertise. I couldn't do it that way. She'd obviously trained the muscles in her face and neck to do all the work. The man moaned. I yawned.

When Steve had come home the night before and told me Cal had invited him to a party, I had been shocked. "So?" I had said. He had shrugged, said he thought we ought to go. I'd asked him why. No reason, he'd said. Just for the fun of it.

Cal's parties stopped being fun for me long before I stopped going. I don't know what happened, but over time, I found myself needing more and more stimulation just to be able to get into them. More booze, more coke, more bodies. It just got to be too much. One night, I extricated my limbs from a tangle of flesh and pulled myself off the king-sized playbed, much to the chagrin of the man who was doing me. "Hey," he yelled. "Where the hell are you going?" I didn't look back, not even sure the clothes I'd picked up off the floor were mine.

After I dressed and went into the living room I realized I didn't have any place to go. Unless it was back to that room in Boyle Heights. Just the thought made me shudder.

That's the night I met Steve. I saw him first through the French doors, hunched over, throwing up all over Cal's prize-winning roses. When he came into the room, he was shaky and sweaty and had to be helped to a chair. I went into the bathroom, got a glass of water, made him drink the whole thing, and then wiped his face and neck with a towel. He thanked me over and over and called me Florence Nightingale. I laughed. He said this was his first party. I wasn't sure just how much "partying" he had done before he got sick, and I didn't ask. He didn't ask me any questions, either.

That was the start of us. I went home with Steve and hadn't been back to the room in Boyle Heights, or to another party.

It felt strange to be back. I'd changed in the last six months; I was falling in love with a guy who built room additions, and it felt good. Lately, I found myself lingering in grocery stores, pondering the superiority of Huggies over Luvs disposable diapers.

When I told Steve I didn't want to go to Cal's party, didn't want to be with those people, he got upset. "Why not?" he said. "Those people were your friends. What's the big deal if we spend a few hours with them?"

"Why do we need to?"

"Damn it, Abby. I work 12 hours a day to keep this business going. Is it a crime to want to relax?"

One of the men in the hot tub pulled himself out of the water and walked over to me. His naked body glistened in the moonlight. "I've been watching you watching them," he said. "Why don't you join us in the tub, gorgeous?"

"Thanks anyway, but I've given up meat for Lent."

He laughed. "Suit yourself. But, if you change your mind, you know where to find me."

The great-room was less crowded when I went back inside, which meant that assignations had been made and people had retired to the various rooms to play out their intentions. Cal had a rule about keeping the sexual activity confined to the bedrooms and the pool area.

Steve wasn't in the bar or around the food table. I went into the library, but he wasn't there, either. The basement had been converted into a movie theater, and many of Cal's guests liked to go down to watch the latest films. Cal had them before they hit the theaters.

Steve was climbing up the stairs from the theater just as I was about to go down.

"Abby, baby! I was coming to find you." His skin was flushed and his eyes held that wild look I'd so often seen in my own. He had done a lot of coke. I smelled liquor on his breath.

The couple behind him was still climbing when he stopped to talk to me, and the girl slammed into his back. Steve turned around and they both giggled. I moved out of the way, and they followed me into the hall. "Baby, I want you to meet my friends. This is…" He giggled again.

"Darla," said the girl.

"Yeah, Darla. And this is…Tom?"

"That's right," Tom said. "Nice to meet you, Abby. Steve's been telling us all about you."

Tom didn't look coked out like his girlfriend, or Steve, did. I nodded my greeting.

"Sweetheart," said Steve, "did I tell you how much I love you and how great I think you are?" He grabbed me around the waist and pulled me to him. His sloppy kiss landed on my chin. I pulled away.

"I think we'd better go home, Steve. You need to come down, sleep it off."

"Bullshit. I feel great, baby. Lots of energy."

Behind him, Darla stifled a giggle. I dropped my voice. "Please, Steve."

His eyes grew dark and his jaw tightened. He wrapped his fingers around my upper arm and pulled me further down the hall, away from his newfound friends.

"Listen, Abby. I'm having a good time. I want to continue having a good time. With them."

I didn't say anything.

"Goddammit, Abby!" His fingers tightened on my arm. "This is fun, that's all. Just a good time."

He was angry, his voice harsh, but there was also a begging quality to it. He sounded like a little kid trying to convince a parent to let him have his way. We'd never discussed Cal's house or his parties after that night we first met. I didn't know if Steve had ever done this kind of scene. I did know he wasn't used to snorting this much coke.

It wasn't as if I'd forgotten what it was like: the coke coursing through my veins making me feel invincible; the freedom inside these impeccable, tastefully decorated walls; the beauty and sensuality of the company filling up my senses; the need to exhaust my energies in every act of pleasure imaginable.

I looked into Steve's eyes. "Is it that important to you? Is it what you really want?"

He let go of my arm. "Yes, Abby. Right here and now, it's what I really want."

Steve's request didn't make me jealous. Instead, I felt empty, defeated. "OK," I said, and walked past him to join Darla and Tom at the end of the hall.

"Why don't you all follow me? I know every room in this house."

"You have beautiful hair," Darla said as she moved it out of the way so that I could snort the lines Tom had set up for me. The coke burned my passages, but it got rid of my headache instantly. "You're very beautiful, Abby."

I leaned back and appraised Darla. "So are you."

She smiled, got up, and began to pull her dress over her head. Static electricity crackled as the fabric passed over her long blond hair, leaving strands of it sticking up into the air. It struck me as funny and I giggled. Darla smoothed her hair down while Tom stood behind her and undid the clasp on her bra. The lace fell away, and he cupped her breasts and rubbed them lightly. She sank back into him, her eyes closed. He whispered in her ear and she smiled, opened her eyes, and walked back to me. Darla leaned over and lightly kissed me on the lips. I looked at Steve. He was taking off his clothes, but watching Darla and me intently. She kissed me again, this time parting my lips with her tongue. I closed my eyes, my mouth opened, and I took in her tongue, sucked at it, concentrating on the feeling I got from its moist softness, a feeling made sharper by the drug racing through my blood. Tom walked up and grabbed Darla's hips. He peeled her panties back and pulled them off. "Why don't we move to the bed?" Darla whispered.

"Sure." I stood up and Darla helped me remove my dress.

Steve took the pillows off the bed, stripped down the blankets, and leaned back against the headboard, his legs tucked under him. I lay flat on my back, my head not far from his lap. He caressed my breasts as Darla's tongue worked the flesh between my midriff and knees. Tiny grunts of pleasure came out of her mouth. Tom, kneeling behind, caressed her and himself as he watched, every few seconds voicing his approval, spurring her on. I looked up into Steve's droopy, lust-laden eyes, felt the excitement he got from watching us jut into the top of my head. "Does this do it for you, baby?" I asked.

"Oh, yeah, Abby. Yeah."

It's funny how the body takes over, how you can suspend your mind and communicate using only your senses. A clitoris doesn't know or care whose tongue or fingers manipulate it. When the hunger peaks and the nerve endings scream, nothing matters.

I gauged time by my thirst and the burning in my nostrils. How much water did I sip? How many lines did I snort? We were all thoroughly immersed in the scene, greedy and sweaty and playing it out, letting the desire rise and fall, rise and fall. At one point, Darla cried out, "What do you think I am, a sex machine?"

"Do you feel like a sex machine?" Tom asked.

"Not nearly enough, goddammit!" The three of them laughed, Steve loudest of all. His laughter found its way past the heat and pleasure that rippled across my body, leaving me cold. "Do you feel like a sex machine, too, Steve?"

"Yeah. And my engine's in fine form." They laughed again.

I sat up, leaned forward on my knees, and brought my face up close to his. "How about letting your vehicle cover some new ground?" I whispered, and then kissed him on the cheek.

"We pretty much covered all of it, baby."

"Not all. You two guys haven't covered all of it." I leaned back, but kept my eyes glued to Steve's. He looked puzzled, but only for a moment, and then attempted a laugh, but it didn't quite make it out of his mouth. I looked at Tom.

"You're kidding, right?" he asked.

Darla yelled, "Hey, what's going on? You guys keeping secrets from me? What are you talking about?" I slid over to Darla and whispered in her ear. Her eyes got wide, and then she threw her head back and laughed. "Yes! You bet. I'd love to see that!"

"You're crazy, Abby," Steve said.

Darla jumped up and down on her knees. "Why is it crazy? I think it's a great idea." She turned to Tom. "Don't you think it's a great idea, Tom?"

Tom glanced at Steve. "Shut up, Darla. Joke's over."

Darla's face got red. She pushed her fist into Tom's shoulder. "A joke, huh? Since when?"

"Darla, I told you to shut up."

Darla ignored him. "He enjoys it. Likes a guy to lick his pee-pee. When was the last time? Six weeks ago?" She reached between his legs and fondled him.

"Why don't we knock off this bullshit?" Steve said. "You know I'm not interested, Abby."

"Really? I don't know anything of the kind. I don't know that much about you at all, do I?"

"Abby—"

"Look at Tom. See how easily he gets hard? Just like you." I grasped Steve's penis and brought my lips up close. I licked the glans, and he hardened against my tongue. I looked up at him, still holding him in my hand. "This is for fun, Steve. It's all for fun. You wanted the experience. Have it. All of it."

"This is enough for me, baby," he said, moving against my fingers.

I let go. "It's not enough for me. I want to watch you with a guy. The way you watched me with Darla. That's what I want."

Darla slid her hand up and down Tom's penis. "Me, too, Tommy. I want to watch, too," she crooned in a baby's voice. "You know you like it."

Tom looked down at Darla's hand moving swiftly against him. He was breathing hard. "Forget it, baby. The guy's not into it. Let's you and me play." He gently pushed Darla's head down into his lap, and she opened her mouth to receive him. He groaned.

I kept my mouth busy, too, working Steve until he sighed with pleasure. I looked up, past Steve, into Darla's eyes, sending her my challenge. After a few moments, she nodded.

Soon, both men were rocking in a steady rhythm; they seemed to be in sync, at the same place, reaching for the same goal. I shot a glance in Darla's direction; she pulled her mouth off Tom and crawled over to Steve and me, ignoring Tom's complaint. I let Steve slip from my mouth and when he protested, I covered his lips with mine. Darla began kissing him on the chest and running her hands over his belly. He tried to push her hand between his legs, but she wouldn't let him. She bit his nipples and slid her fingers over his groin, deliberately missing his penis. He moaned, sucked harder on my tongue. I pulled away and looked at Tom. He was pulling on his penis, his mouth hanging open. "Come here," I said. He crawled over to us on his hands and knees. "Touch him."

Steve made an attempt to object, but I covered his mouth with mine again. He relaxed against me at the same moment that Tom's head brushed past my belly and dove between Steve's legs. For a moment, Steve's body stiffened, and then he relaxed again. Darla sustained her licking and pinching; I kept the kiss going, moved it from his lips to his neck, to the nipple free of Darla's mouth, all the way down to where Tom's lips smacked against his hardened flesh. My tongue joined Tom's, and together we licked and sucked until Steve began to pant.

I knew his body so well. Knew how much he could take, what would speed him up or slow him down, finish him or keep him teetering on the edge. The measure of his breath, the depth of his sighs, the whimper stuck in his throat let me know when to pull back, to sustain his pleasure or increase his agony. My hands squeezed, fingers pinched, held back his flood until the blood beating in his veins calmed, and when it did, Tom came at him, his mouth an instrument of pleasant torment, forcing Steve to start the ascent again. Above us, Darla gently kissed his face, his eyes, licked his ears, sucked at his chin while her painted fingernails flicked the tip of each nipple.

Together, we teased Steve into a frenzy; his features became blurred from sweat pouring from his body. He thrashed about, seeking release, but we held him with the power of our circling tongues, the canopy of our curved torsos, the strength of our determined limbs. Pinned beneath us clutching blindly, spasmodically, he cried out, begged us to bring him off, but we answered him with lips that grazed his penis, palms that buffed his thighs, fingers that hummed against his anus.

"Enough," he shouted, "enough!" But we didn't stop, in fact, increased the tempo until his breaths became shorter, his movements faster, and I feared that he would waste himself just to be done with our exquisite torture. I signaled Darla and Tom to stop what they were doing, pressed close to Steve's steamy body, and licked the sweat from his brow.

He turned his head to look at me. "God, Abby, you're driving me crazy!"

"Tell me again how much you love me, Steve," I whispered into his ear.

"I do...Fuck me, Abby..."

"I want you to feel as much pleasure as you can, baby. I want you to climb the highest mountain before I push you off."

"Push me off now, Abby...I'm so ready to be pushed off the

goddamned mountain!"

"All right, baby. My way?"

"Any way, Abby.... Please."

I nodded and slipped off the bed, tiptoed to the closet, and reached inside. One could always count on Cal to keep a plentiful supply of restraints for anyone interested in such devices. These particular ropes were made of strong, yet soft, leather.

I trailed the leather over Steve's chest and engorged penis. He shuddered. "I want to go for a ride," I said. "You, in the dark. All right, baby?" I didn't wait for his answer, but leaned over and tongued him deeply. He attempted to reach up to wrap his arms around me, but his body shook, weakened by desire. "A long, hard ride into an exploding sunset."

He sighed.

Darla and Tom had been quietly watching our exchange. I tossed one of the leather ties to Tom, and he secured Steve's left arm to the headboard while Darla helped me with his other arm. Then I put the blindfold on him. "In the dark," I repeated. "You love it in the dark, don't you?"

He murmured his answer as I straddled him, rubbing my wet sex slowly over his chest, inching up in increments until I reached his mouth. His tongue entered me and I moved my hips upward, letting it slide out. Then, as if in slow motion, I came back down until only the tip of his tongue was inside. I hovered there for a moment, while he strained his neck, trying to gain access to more of me. I let him in, but only a fraction of an inch, and then backed off. He cried out, yelled my name in protest, and I promised that soon he would experience the most astounding orgasm of his life.

Steve pulled against his restraints, his fingers curling, clawing the air, and he raised his legs in an attempt to grab me. There was no way he could. I kept my sex dancing over his mouth, but never close enough to satisfy his hunger. As I moved, I fondled my breasts and held Tom's eyes. He watched me, tugged at his penis until it was long and hard, and then murmured for Darla to get on her knees.

"No!" I scrambled off Steve, grabbed Darla's panties from the floor, and stuffed them into his mouth. Then I tossed the remaining ties to Tom and told him to turn Steve over. He hesitated. I looked at Darla. She had taken hold of my excitement. Her eyes wide, her breath labored, she stepped up to Tom, picked up the ties, and slapped them across his face. "Yes!" she shouted. "Yes!" A signal passed between them. Tom reached across her and grabbed Steve's leg, pulled it tight, and tugged. There was sufficient slack in his wrist ties to twist them so that they gave enough to let us turn his body over.

Behind the gag, he screamed. He kicked at us, making it difficult to keep hold of his legs, but after a while we managed to secure both legs to the footboard.

Exhausted, I stood back and surveyed the "X" Steve's body made across the bed, his muscles pulled taut and shiny with sweat. Seeing him spread-eagled, unable to move, stirred a desire within me I didn't know I possessed. I climbed onto his back, pressed myself to his body, my arms spread over his, my legs splayed like his. "I dreamed a different dream, but it didn't come true."

On my knees between his legs, I bent to kiss the cheeks of his ass, to gently bite and lick them. My hand caressed his scrotum lightly. Steve still fought, thrashing against the sweat-soaked sheet, but I kept up my kisses, kept petting his heavy sac lightly with my fingers until his hips rolled into the mattress and his penis was shiny with his juice. His cries behind the gag had quieted to soft moans. I spread his cheeks and wet my finger, pressed lightly on the folds of puckered skin, and stroked his opening, gently escalating the rhythm until his body opened to the pleasure.

I looked back to see Darla and Tom on the floor, her mouth closed over him, drawing at him heartily. He grabbed her head and pulled until all I could see were his balls touching her chin. "Darla!" At the harsh tone of my voice, she drew her mouth away. Darla looked up at Tom. "Fuck him," she said. He didn't answer. "Go on...fuck him in his gorgeous virgin ass, Tom. His tight, beautiful ass."

Tom licked his lips, pulled himself off the floor, and walked over to the bed. He lifted his penis, slick with Darla's saliva, and motioned for me to move out of the way. I slipped off the bed and Tom took my place.

Steve lay very still—in terror or anticipation, I couldn't tell. Tom rubbed himself along the crack of Steve's ass, and I yanked the panties out of his mouth. "Don't do this, Abby," he said. His eyes pleaded with me, the fear in them unmistakable. Still, his ass quivered each time Tom rimmed his opening. Yes, I thought, it's funny how the body takes over. His own balls and cock were full. I knew what it was he feared.

"Ram it into him!"

Tom burrowed into Steve's body with several powerful thrusts. He gritted his teeth and cried out as he worked himself deeper and deeper inside Steve's ass. "Ah...so sweet, so sweet," he mumbled, lost in the sensation of this brand of fucking.

"God! He's something, isn't he? I love when he gets going like this!" said Darla.

Steve howled, bucked backward into Tom, his cries a mixture of pain and pleasure. I spread my legs and slipped my fingers over my swollen clit.

Tom pulled back, slid his penis nearly all the way out, and then rammed into Steve with such force that his eyes rolled back in his head. He grasped Steve's hips and fucked him with increasing fervor.

The man who had earlier said he loved me, told me how great he thought I was, screamed my name, flung filthy epithets at me as the evidence of his gratification splattered against the sheet. At the same time, the confirmation of mine gushed against my fingers. When it was over, Tom slipped to the floor and lay panting on the rug. Steve pressed his face into the mattress. His shoulders shook as he wept.

Soft breath against my ear broke my concentration. Darla held me around the waist and fondled my breasts. I pulled my gaze off Steve and pushed her away.

"Hey—"

"Get out," I screamed. "Both of you. Get the hell out!"

"Fucking maniac," Darla said, but she scurried around gathering their fallen garments. I kicked Tom in his side, told him to get up and get out. He rolled over and pulled himself up. He didn't say a word.

Kneeling at the head of the bed, I ran my fingers through Steve's hair, massaged the muscles in his neck, and crooned soothing words to him. Inside the bathroom, Tom and Darla hurried into their clothes. I stopped paying attention and didn't hear them leave.

Steve continued to whimper, and I cried, too, my face pressed up against his, our tears mingling together. I kept smoothing his hair, murmuring softly into his ear until his body relaxed and he fell asleep. He lay like a rock, snoring soundly, oblivious as I removed the straps and rubbed his ankles and wrists. Light filtered around the edges of the heavy drapes at the windows, announcing a new day.

Later, I stood at the foot of the bed, watching Steve sleep. In another part of the house, Cal and his boys would be waking up, waiting to be served breakfast. I wondered who would be doing the cooking. I'd ask Cal if he'd let me crack the eggs, and then I'd ask him if he really, really missed me.

RATATOUILLE

Susannah Indigo

"MILES, DID YOU KNOW THAT ZUCCHINIS MAKE
the best cocks?" Isabelle asked me on our first date.
She twirled her angel-hair pasta and looked fondly
at the veggie stabbed on the end of her fork.

She had my attention. I tried to guess at a
good response. Isabelle had long, wavy red hair
and dancer's legs, and there wasn't much I
wouldn't consider for her.

"Better than cucumbers?" I asked rather
dumbly but with great gusto, as though we were
discussing favorite recipes over the back fence.

She laughed. "Hell, yes. Better than men,
sometimes. Better than vibrators, always. No
batteries, and much more organic."

I was speechless. I had watched Isabelle pass
by my office for weeks on the way to the dance
studio before I found the nerve to ask her out. I
was developing a serious navy-blue leg-warmer

fetish by the time I just stepped into the hall and blurted out my name and invited her to dinner.

"Sure, Miles," she had said, quite casually. "But it has to be vegetarian for me, OK?"

She had looked pure and angelic with that pale white skin and the sprinkling of freckles across her nose. I researched every health food restaurant in town.

"Organic is good," I finally answered her at dinner, feeling like a 16-year-old kid on his first date instead of the lawyer that I was. "Do you peel the zucchini?" I had to know.

"Sometimes, Miles," she answered. "But sometimes rougher is better, you know?"

I thought then that maybe it was possible to fall in love with a girl who said "you know?" all the time and who wore heavy silver rings and bracelets that weighed her down, bracelets that looked like handcuffs on her delicate wrists.

I took her home to her tiny walk-up apartment at the top of an old building not far from Coors Field. "This neighborhood is not safe," I told her.

She just laughed at me. "Life is not safe, darling."

She was right, of course. There's hardly any safety in hating what you do every day for a living. When I chose law school over art so long ago, I didn't know the difference between financial security and being safe.

She invited me in and lit six black candles all around the room "Six," she informed me," is the sacred number of Aphrodite, the goddess of love." She served me hot tea on an elegant silver tray and then looked straight into my eyes and told me how it was going to be.

"A girl has to have rules, you know," she said. "I never have full sex with a man until the third date." She smiled. "By then I can always tell if they're fuckable or not."

I was 37 years old and a man of the world when she said this, and I swear I couldn't remember ever having sex before in my life, or if I even knew how.

"That sounds fair," I mumbled, smoothing my hair.

She excused herself and went to the bathroom. I confess I sneaked a look in her fridge while she was gone. Never before had a crisper looked so sexy. I counted the zucchinis—there were six. All in a row.

She came back, and her hair was tied up and she pressed one of her strong legs next to mine on the futon. Without a word she picked up a jar of honey from the tea tray, stuck her finger into it, and smeared honey all over her lips. Honey over lipstick, honey around her mouth, honey on her tongue, never taking her eyes off mine.

She stopped. "Kiss me, Miles. Kiss me until all my honey is gone."

Dear god. I started with a lick and then I was devouring her, and nothing else existed but Isabelle and her mouth. Long, soulful kisses that went on forever, or maybe it was just one kiss that kept inventing itself over and over and over until I thought her rules were only a tease and my hand was high on her thigh and my cock was raving wild. She paused and whispered, "You kiss like a man who is hungry. This is a good thing." And then she kicked me out the door.

I bought her things. I showed up for the second date with flowers and candy and a gift of tiny, delicate crystal ballet slippers that reminded me of her. She laughed and thanked me, but later she told me that the things she wanted in life couldn't be bought.

She was wearing a shiny white leotard, the kind with long sleeves that looked as if it would fall off her shoulders any minute, the kind you can see nipples through in the right light, and a long, swirling, deep-blue skirt that made me want to lift it and bend her over and fuck her hard and fast. But it was only the second date, and rules are rules.

"Are you a natural redhead?" I asked, admiring her hair.

"You'll never know, darling. Don't you know that dancers wax everywhere but their heads?" She laughed and lifted her skirt, slid the leotard aside, and twirled and flashed me the loveliest bare pussy I will ever see in my life.

And then she led me out the door to the theater.

We saw *Cats*. She made me. She kept my hand high on her thigh under her skirt the whole time. I was wrong: *Cats* is a wonderful show.

Back at her place, she asked if I was hungry. I believe the exact words were "What are you hungry for?"

The possibilities raced through my head. "Oh, something vegetarian," I said casually, still trying to impress.

Her eyes lit up. "I have lots of fresh veggies in my crisper. Let's marinate some of them before we cook."

She took me into the kitchen. We peeled. Two zucchinis, three carrots, a handful of mushrooms, and a large purple onion. "The living room is better for this," she whispered when we were finished with our plate.

Lavender-scented candles, incense, the aroma of fresh zucchini—these smells will stay with me all of my life. She turned on the music, stretched out on the tiny rug on the hardwood floor, took off her leotard, and lifted that blue skirt around her waist and asked me if I wanted to watch or to help. I could barely move; I said I would love to watch her. I touched the pale skin high between her thighs and petted her gently as if she were a kitten; she closed her eyes and threw her head back and showed me possibilities I didn't know existed. She loved that vegetable as if it were a cock, stroking herself with it, rubbing it slowly around her clit, entering her pussy slowly, so slowly, in and out, teasing me, teasing herself, and then finally fucking herself hard—my cock beat right to her rhythm. I came when she came; I came in my pants as if I was 15 again. She was lying back on the floor and I kissed her pussy, I kissed that cock, and I kissed her legs from thigh to ankle over and over again.

And then we cooked.

Stir-fry veggies over tomato-basil pasta; peppermint tea; fortune cookies. It was an extraordinary meal—I suspect it was the special sauce. "You will attend a royal banquet and meet your first lover," my fortune cookie said, and I knew I just had.

She changed into a little-girl flannel nightgown and took me into her bed. We slept. No sex. The trust implicit in this act was overwhelming. I never touched her except to hold her tight.

In the morning we laughed together. "Carrots just don't quite work, you know?" she said. "Too thin. But they have some uses. Eggplants and tomatoes and onions and peppers all have uses sometimes too." She told me that her practice was as old as the Kama Sutra: "How else do you think all those women in the harems got satisfied? Hell, that book even goes into using the root of the sweet potato! Sometimes," she confessed, almost blushing, "I go out with something inside me, when I'm going someplace quiet like the museum. It makes you think about sex all day. Melon balls are my favorite—kind of an organic set of Ben Wa balls."

If this was foreplay, I wasn't sure I was ready for full sex. I went to see her dance on the third date. She was beautiful. We went back to her place, and I lit the candles and the incense. "I'm yours tonight," she whispered. "You've passed. What would you like?"

I was ready. What else could a man want? "I want you to love me, to worship me just like you did that zucchini."

She undressed me while I stood there, and then she knelt in front of me and began. It all came back to me in that moment, why sex is the most important damned thing in the world. She kissed my feet and then she worked her way up, taking forever, kissing and licking my balls and holding them gently in her mouth. Talking to me, saying things, telling me how good I tasted, telling me how much she wanted me inside her, how much she needed to ride me hard. She took my cock deep into her throat all at once, and then there were no rules or they were only my rules and she was mine and I was lying back and holding her small hips and lifting her up onto my cock and driving up into her hard and fast. The world stopped; that was all I knew—that she could make the outside world stop and take me back to where I belonged. She came for me over and over, before I stopped and took her long hair in my fist and held her still for a minute.

"Do you want to please me?" I whispered, knowing that she did, knowing that this girl lived for sex and that I could give her what she needed.

"God, yes," she whispered, nodding.

"Turn over."

I owned her. I fucked every part of her body, and she begged for more. I couldn't quite imagine matching her sexual imagination, but I discovered I could more than match her energy and desire. When my cock was finally deep in her ass and my own vision of heaven was high on the horizon, I suddenly knew: I knew this was it and this girl was going to change my life. I didn't tell her this; I thought there would be time later.

I don't believe we slept that night. But I do know that I never let her near the kitchen.

I started drawing again. I sketched her constantly. I still have some of the drawings—"Isabelle in Iceberg" is my favorite one, framed on my wall. Even though she swore the lettuce just didn't do a thing for her.

I stopped eating meat. Isabelle—her name in my mouth was better than any sirloin in town.

I went dancing with her. I don't dance. Little clubs that nobody my age has ever heard of; dark entrances, pounding music, Isabelle twirling and twirling and always coming back to my arms.

She let me go to the beauty parlor with her and watch her get waxed all over. I only went because she told me she loved it, loved the pain, loved the discipline of it all. "Discipline is everything in dance," she told me.

I would ask her to show me her pussy and she would. Any time. She danced for me whenever I wanted. I wouldn't call it stripping, but I guess that's what it was. And the world would stop one more time.

But when I wasn't with her, she would rarely answer the phone, and I just *knew* she was in bed with a zucchini, and I couldn't stand it. She'd see me once a week—that was all—and I knew the girl was getting fucked every day.

I got stupid like men do. I followed her—saw her at the produce stand, watched her dancing through the studio window, saw her go out with friends and then go home alone. I knew there was no other man. When I asked her, she told me she'd been in love once and that was enough.

She liked me; I knew she did. And then I realized the problem. It still pains me to admit it. She preferred her vegetables over me, just as she had told me on that first date. How on earth can a man compete with an edible cock?

I couldn't get past once a week, and summer was running down and I wanted Isabelle in my bed every night. She wasn't a tease. There was no game. God, how she could fuck. Some nights she would just lift her skirt and wiggle her ass onto my lap, pressing down hard on my cock before we'd even go out. She'd tell me how much she needed my cock. "It's my real kink," she confessed, "just being penetrated. Everywhere."

I tried to force the issue. I asked her outright what the story was, why we couldn't spend more time together. "Trust all joy," she'd say mysteriously, and then she'd wrap her hair around my cock and take me in her throat until I forgot even what the question was. "You taste wonderful since you stopped eating meat," she'd whisper after she'd swallowed and licked me clean. She was very into taste. "You taste like cinnamon, you taste like a perfect cup of hot chocolate on a cold winter night," and somehow I knew this was true and nobody had ever noticed it before.

Saturday nights were heaven. By Tuesday I'd be going crazy. I moaned, I fretted. I knew I was driving her nuts with my demands but I couldn't stop. I studied myself in the mirror and contemplated my fuckability factor. When you're in competition with a vegetable, every little bit helps.

Other women called me and I simply had no interest. "Isabelle"—her name in my mouth was more appealing than an onion.

What could I do? Move her to the country and give her a farm? Buy out a local produce stand? I couldn't imagine. I studied her apartment. All she owned was cheap furniture and beautiful candles and scarves and one shelf each of music and books. "I used to own a lot more," she told me when I asked, "but then I learned that possessions mean nothing. So now I read a book and then just pass it on to a friend for their pleasure. The same with music, unless it feeds my soul. I pass it on." There were no clues about how to get to her. So I got stupider. I bribed her grocer to tell me every single thing she bought each trip. Six-inch zukes, bunches of carrots, scallions...scallions? I had to do something.

One Saturday night, late in August, I tried joining forces with the produce. I used them to fuck her every which way, and it was hot and satisfying, but I was still relegated to Saturday night while they got the other six. I got jealous. I hoped they would wilt under the pressure.

I decided to try an intervention. There are no support groups for this kind of thing. She canceled our date one Saturday night, and I knew I'd never make it another week without her. I laid the plan for Tuesday night: I would simply show up, lock the door, and clean out her fridge. I knew if I could spend enough time with her I could somehow make her replace her veggie vice with me. I certainly knew I could measure up: I'd spent one night with a ruler and tape measure back near the beginning of stupid.

I knocked on her door that Tuesday night and there was no answer; it pushed open easily. She was gone. No books, no candles, no music, no Isabelle. I could picture her in front of me twirling and laughing in that blue skirt; but when I reached out to touch her, there was nothing but ordinary space. I believe I stood there for close to forever; the world may have even stopped for me one last time.

Then I checked the fridge. It was empty except for one zucchini with a note wrapped around it: "I've gone on tour, darling," it said. "Pass it on."

TARA ALTON'S erotica has appeared in *Clean Sheets, Scarlet Letters, Playgirl,* and *Variations.* She lives in the Midwest where she works as a travel consultant. When she's not working or writing, she collects tattoos, worships Bette Page, and plans new adventures.

JENESI ASH'S stories have been published in *My Sister's Secret Place, Dare,* and *Zaftig!* As Joli Agnew, her stories are in *Bordello, Gay Black Female, KUMA,* and *The Sapphic Muse.* She would like to thank Hanne Blank for her insights on "Santa's Little Helper."

J.L. BELROSE'S fiction and poetry have appeared in *Lezzie Smut, Siren, Quota,* and *Queer View Mirror.* Her stories will appear in three upcoming Alyson anthologies: *Skin Deep, Pillow Talk II,* and *Uniform Sex.* She lives in Ontario, and has just completed her first novel.

HANNE BLANK is columns editor of *Scarlet Letters,* and writes regularly for *Clean Sheets, Paramour, Black Sheets, Anything That Moves,* and *The Televisionary Oracle.* Her book *Big Big Love: A Sourcebook on Sex for People of Size and Those Who Love Them* will be published in early 2000 by Greenery Press.

CARA BRUCE is a senior editor at GettingIt.com and the editor of *Venus or Vixen?* (www.venusorvixen.com). Her stories have appeared in *The Unmade Bed, The Oy of Sex, Uniforms,* and *Best Lesbian Erotica 2000.* She is also editor of *Viscera,* a compilation of bizarre erotica.

KATE DOMINIC is a Los Angeles–based writer addicted to sexy stories. Her work has been published under various pen names. She received honorable mention in *Libido* magazine's 1997 fiction contest. "The Album" was published in *Herotica 6,* an erotica anthology on the theme of committed relationships.

AMELIA G is editor of *Blue Blood* magazine. Her stories have appeared in *Eros Ex Machina, Best American Erotica 2000,* and *Playboy* online.

SUSANNAH INDIGO'S fiction is published on Erotasy (www.Erotasy.com), in *Libido, Black Sheets, Howlings: Wild Women of the West, Herotica 6,* and *Best American Erotica 2000.*

EMMA HOLLY has published a number of erotic novels. Her favorite inspirations are long walks, late mornings, and a ready supply of chocolate.

RANDI KREGER takes her first stab at writing fiction with "Strange Bedfellows." She is primarily a nonfiction writer and has cowritten the self-help book *Stop Walking on Eggshells.* She maintains a World Wide Web site for people who care about someone with borderline personality disorder (www.BPD.Central.com), the topic of her book. Her "real-life job" is that of a public relations and marketing consultant in Milwaukee.

KATHERINE LOVE studies music in New York City. This year will mark her first published story and her first legal drink.

MARYANNE MOHANRAJ edits cleansheets.com, a website for cutting-edge erotica. She is consulting editor for *Herotica 7* and author of *Torn Shapes of Desire*. Her work also appears in *Sex Toy Tales* and in *Best American Erotica 1999*.

LESLÉA NEWMAN has published some 30 books, including *Pillow Talk: Lesbian Stories Between the Covers (Volumes I and II); The Little Butch Book; The Femme Mystique; My Lover Is a Woman: Contemporary Lesbian Love Poems; Out of the Closet and Nothing to Wear;* and *Heather Has Two Mommies.* Her website is www.lesleanewman.com. "Eggs McMenopause" is taken from her new book of fiction, *Girls Will Be Girls.*

LISA PROSIMO lives in Southern California where she is hard at work editing biographies for a digital library. Her erotic short stories have appeared in Lonnie Barbach's *Seductions, Herotica 6,* and *Sauce*Box Journal.*

JEAN ROBERTA lives in one of the world's most extreme climates, on the Canadian prairie. She teaches English at the local university and is active in the feminist and gay rights movements. She has won awards for fiction, and her poems and articles have been published widely in magazines and anthologies.

SUSAN ST. AUBIN's writing has appeared in diverse journals and anthologies, among them *The Reed, Magazine, Short Story Review, Yellow Silk, Libido,* the *Herotica* series, and *Best American Erotica 1995* and *2000.* She is an administrative support coordinator by day and a pornographer by night.

LISA VERDE is a writer and Web production director living outside Chicago, with her husband and their two children. For three years Lisa was editor of the literary magazine *Pica*. Her short fiction has appeared in *B&A New Fiction, Oasis,* and Erotasy.com. She was a runner-up in the *Story* Short Short Story contest in 1998. Her favorite nail polish brands are OPI, Hard Candy, and Sinful.

KRISTINA WRIGHT is a freelance writer and book reviewer for *Literary Times*. Her erotic fiction has been published by Silhouette Books, and she is a staff writer for Custom Erotica Source (www.customerotica.com).

MARCY SHEINER is editor of *The Oy of Sex: Jewish Women's Erotica* (Cleis Press) and of *Herotica 4, 5,* and 6 (Plume; Down There Press). She is also erotica editor for ThePosition.com, the Website of The Museum of Sex. Her stories and essays have appeared in many anthologies and publications. She is currently writing a novel.